CHAPTER 1

ALICIA CRUZ couldn't remember the last time she'd had her friends over for a sleepover. They'd pretty much given up on them in the eighth grade. Which isn't to say they hadn't hung out all night long until the break of dawn ever since—not only in their hometown of Miami, but as far away as Spain. Sometimes they hung out for fun, like in the ninth grade, when for Alicia's fifteenth birthday, she had passed on the traditional Sweet Fifteen extravaganza, known the world over as a *quinceañera*, and instead traveled to Spain with her pal Carmen Ramirez-Ruben. In Barcelona, restaurants didn't even start serving dinner until nine, so Alicia and her parents and Carmen had dined many times at midnight and explored the Rambla, the heart of the city, as they strolled back to the hotel.

Two years ago, the late-night sessions had become more focused on work, when Alicia's desire to do a good deed and help a new girl in town plan her *quinceañera* turned into a full-blown business, Amigas Incorporated. And so, while Alicia had never had a *quince* of her own, she had now planned and attended dozens of them. She ran Amigas Inc. with Carmen and her other best friend and partner, Jamie Sosa. Now the three girls sat at the helm of the hottest teen-party-planning business in town—with a substantial company bank account and a very snazzy Young Entrepreneurs of Miami Award from the mayor's office to prove it.

Over the last couple of years, they'd spent many nights creating the most magical details for their clients. Alicia could hardly remember how many times she'd stayed up all night while Carmen, who was an ace seamstress and an amazing designer, put the finishing touches on a *quince* ball gown. They had all watched the sun rise from Jamie's studio, a garage turned working-artist's space, while Jamie completed a mural or a video project that took an already awesome celebration right over the top.

There wasn't anything you could tell Alicia and her girls about working hard. They'd all been there— blood, sweat, and tears—which was why Alicia wanted to have a sleepover. Lately, it seemed that every time they got together, it was a business meeting—everybody with their iPads out, diligently taking notes and penciling in dates. She missed having a simple girls' night in, with lots of good food, a cheesy DVD to laugh at, and nothing to do but relax and have a good time.

The doorbell rang, and Alicia knew it was Jamie, a dark-skinned Latina whose family originally came from the Dominican Republic. Having grown up in the Bronx, Jamie had been all hard edges and attitude. Then she fell in love with Dash Mortimer, the half Venezuelan, half American aristocrat and all-hottie golf player, and it rocked her world. Though it had taken a while for Jamie to reconcile the notion of herself as a girl from the streets with that of the girl who now hung out at country clubs and took private planes on the regular, the change had been good for her. Dash taught Jamie that she didn't have to be hard to be real.

Jamie now strutted into the Cruz family home in a slouchy charcoal cashmere sweater, leopard-print leggings, and sky-high heels. Alicia couldn't help laughing a little. "Come on, *chica*, I'm as fashion-forward as the next girl, but did you have to get so fancy for a sleepover?"

Jamie kicked her shoes off. "Ooooh, *mami*, I just had an early dinner with Dash. He was in town for an

ESPN event last night, but he has to get back to Duke. I wanted to look cute—make sure I kept my edge over all those boy-crazy college girls."

In addition to crisscrossing the country on the junior PGA circuit, Dash Mortimer was a freshman at Duke University. Jamie had spent most of the summer trying to break up with him in anticipation of what she called "the inevitable," but Dash had finally convinced her that distance wasn't going to be their undoing. "It's over when it's over," he had told her one night after she picked another fight with him. Pulling her toward him for a kiss that seemed to last forever, he had said, "I don't know about you, but this doesn't feel like it's ever going to be over." It was only the last week of September, still early in the semester, and so far the unlikely couple was holding strong.

The doorbell rang again, and now Carmen joined them. Although she was the group's designated fashionista, she was dressed—as Alicia was—in sleepover-ready gear: an off-the-shoulder sweatshirt, black leggings, and neon pink fuzzy socks.

"Pajama party!" Carmen said, giving each of her friends the Latin *doble* kiss—a peck on each cheek. Carmen was Chicana on her mother's side, Jewish Argentinean on her father's side, and as she liked to say, she wasn't half and half, she was one hundred percent Latina.

As the girls tucked in to a meal of takeout Indian—samosas, rice, and spicy chicken vindaloo—the conversation drifted to the big question mark on the horizon: college.

"So, Lici, is that T-shirt a sign of your coming around?" Jamie asked playfully. "All that ivy looks good on you."

Alicia was wearing a maroon and yellow Harvard T-shirt. Her parents had met at Harvard, and they'd made no secret of the fact that it would make them positively ecstatically happy if Alicia followed in their footsteps by attending that venerable institution.

Alicia blushed. "I just like wearing it, that's all."

Carmen tore off a piece of the Indian bread called naan and dipped it in the raita, a yogurt and cucumber dip that was the perfect cooling complement to the spicier dishes.

"And the fact that Gaz could be right down the road at Berklee doesn't have anything to do with it?" Carmen asked.

Berklee College of Music had one of the top programs in the country for aspiring musicians, and

Alicia's boyfriend and sometime *quince* collaborator, Gaz Colón, was a *serious* musician. He didn't just play in a high school garage band, he'd already signed a deal with an independent label in Nashville. They hadn't placed any of his tunes yet, but Alicia had no doubt that one of Gaz's sweet and sexy love songs would have audiences cheering in the rafters and would be playing on a million iPods sooner or later.

She loved him. She adored his music. She just wasn't sure how much she should let her relationship influence what felt like the most important decision of her life.

"I don't know," Alicia replied, feeling uncharacteristically nervous and uncertain. "Don't you guys think it's lame to choose a school based on where your boyfriend is going to college?"

Jamie held up one finger and gave Alicia a little South Bronx head swivel. "Oh, come on, *chica*. When that school is Harvard, the most prestigious university in da world, the answer is no, it's not lame."

"But it's where my parents went. It's where my boyfriend wants me to go. There's no *me* in that equation." Alicia rested her head on Carmen's shoulder. "You understand, right, C.?"

Carmen patted her friend's arm reassuringly, just the way she had when Alicia had gotten food poisoning the time they all went to Key West to plan a *quince* for a very eccentric girl who lived in a house full of three-legged cats.

"Alicia," Carmen replied, "you're large and in charge. It's not what you choose to do, it's who you are. And you'll be running the joint, with a pile of friends and fans, wherever you go."

Alicia looked reassured; she always was when Carmen gave her advice. It wasn't just that Carmen was her oldest friend—which she was—it was also that Carmen had the mellow vibe of a Zen yoga master.

"Thanks, C.," Alicia said. "What about you guys? Things all moving along according to plan?"

"I'm trying to keep it simple," Jamie answered. "I'm planning to apply to three colleges in my favorite city, which, of course, is NYC. To mix things up a bit, I'm also looking at two schools with great graphic-design departments: Savannah College of Art and Design, and there's a dual program at Brown and Rhode Island School of Design."

"I'm going to apply to twelve colleges," Carmen said, smiling, "which seems like eight too many, but when your mom teaches high school, going above and beyond is the name of the game. Then we'll see where I get in and what I can afford. My dad's latest *telenovela*,

¡Qué Lástima!, just went into syndication in twenty-two countries, so *Papá* says if I get into almost anywhere, he'll cover the tuition, so I should be okay."

"What about 'To the Max' Maxo?" Jamie said. "Boyfriend have any preferences?"

Maxo was Carmen's new "guyfriend," as she called him. They'd gotten to know each other at the end of junior year. Alicia and Jamie liked to call him "To the Max" Maxo, because he was cute—to the max; smart—to the max; and sweet—well, to the max.

Carmen smiled. "Maxo is actually going to take a year off to work with the Geekcorps in Haiti. He's going to be part of a volunteer IT team that helps local communities become more proficient in information and communications technologies."

"See?" Jamie laughed. "He's even a do-gooder—to the max."

"And you'll be okay with him being in another country for a whole year?" Alicia wondered.

Carmen shrugged, "Are you kidding? The rebuilding effort down there will take *years*, if not decades. I'm so proud of him for being willing to sacrifice a year to make a difference. I'll miss him, just like I'll miss you guys. But I want everyone I love to follow their dreams, no matter where they take them."

"You're awesome, Carm. I wish I could be as relaxed and mature as you are about this senior-year decision-making stuff," Alicia said as she put down her fork. "What I love about *quinceañeras* is that they are all about ritual and transition. You turn fifteen. You go to a church and the priest blesses you. You change from flat shoes to high heels. Presto change-o, you're no longer a kid, you're a woman. Then you have a big party and you dance the night away. Why can't finishing high school be like that?"

Jamie and Carmen both raised their eyebrows. Alicia very rarely had meltdowns. But when she did, they tended to be epic—and the girls had a feeling that deep in their friend's heart, a meltdown of legendary proportions was brewing.

"Sweetie," Carmen offered, "there's a process for finishing high school. It's called graduation."

Jamie reached for Alicia's *quince* crown and added, "You even get to wear a funny hat. There are speeches and a formal ceremony, just like in a *quince*. And there are huge parties after."

Alicia did not look satisfied. "But that comes when all the hard work is done, when you've taken your SATs, applied to colleges, and actually decided where you want to go. The difficult part is now, when there's a million decisions to make and each one feels way significant." Biting the straw in her drink, she said, "You know what I wish?"

Jamie shook her head. "I have no idea."

Carmen shrugged. "Not a clue."

"I wish there were an equivalent of us, an Amigas Inc., to guide you through the whole process—from college tours to SATs to applications and decision making."

Jamie reached into her purse for a tube of lip gloss. "Uh, *duh*. There is. It's called guidance counselors."

Alicia shook her head. "See, that's like saying regular party-planners are like us. If only there were girls who'd just been through it—who could help you decide."

Carmen knew then that her friend was really scared, not just about whether or not she'd go to Harvard, but about all the other changes that lay ahead, too. "Lici," she said tenderly, "*no te preocupes*. We'll help each other through this. We'll do what we always do when we plan a *quince*. We'll make a checklist. We'll divide the tasks according to our strengths, and we'll rock it out. Just like we always do."

"Pinkie promise?" Alicia said, extending a little finger to each of her best friends.

The girls locked fingers.

"There's only one thing that could make me feel even better," Alicia said shyly.

"And what's that?" Carmen asked, glad that her friend seemed to have been talked down from the ledge.

"If Jamie would lend me her mad hot shoes. They are fabulous, and they are spanking new. Not like mine, which are cute, but hand-me-downs from my mom." Alicia slipped the shoes on and ran out into the hall. She was quite a sight in her worn-out Harvard T, navy cutoffs, and runway-ready patent-leather heels.

"I got those shoes on eBay," Jamie said, running after her.

"Of course you did," Alicia grinned. Jamie's prowess at finding incredible deals online was legendary.

"They come from a seller in Antwerp," Jamie added as she caught up to Alicia. "That style never even came to the US."

Alicia took the shoes off and tossed one to Carmen. "Feel that leather, Carmen. It's like buttah," she laughed.

Jamie stood between Alicia and Carmen, desperately trying to catch one of her shoes as they sailed over her head. "You do know that you're playing hot potato with a very exquisite pair of heels, don't you?" she asked.

"And to think," Alicia said innocently, "back in the eighth grade, we played hot potato with real potatoes. What a bore!" Then she dissolved in giggles, relieved that, although as seniors in high school they were too old for many things, sleepovers weren't among them.

CHAPTER 2

THE NEXT MØRNING, Alicia and her friends gathered at the snack bar of the quad outside their school, Coral Gables High. C. G. High was located in one of Miami's most luxurious residential neighborhoods. Even though September in Miami was plenty warm, the girls had shifted from their summer uniforms of strapless dresses, flip-flops, and sandals into the long cardigans, leggings, and knee-high boots that signaled the onset of fall and the beginning of the school year.

As they sipped various drinks, they were greeted by students they barely knew. They smiled and waved hello, feeling sometimes a little like reality TV stars. Like it or not, if you build a business throwing the hottest *quinceañeras* in town, you're more than just popular, you're kinda famous.

Rafael, a cute and incredibly built guy who was

captain of the swimming team, called out to them, "Hey, *chicas*, when's the next bangin' birthday party?"

Jamie smiled sweetly and said, "Wow, I wish I could tell you, but that's not how this works. You actually have to be invited by the birthday girl to the party."

Rafael grinned. "See, that's why y'all need to open up a club or something."

Jamie laughed, "A club? Um, we're just trying to get into college."

"I hear that," Rafael agreed, holding up his hand for a high five. Jamie gave him some dap, and before he walked away, he said, "Have a nice day, ladies. Try to slip me an invite for your next shindig."

As they watched him leave, Carmen said, "Remember when we were freshmen? We would have just *melted* if a guy like Rafael ever talked to us."

Jamie agreed. "Now we've all got boyfriends."

Carmen nodded. "Really awesome boyfriends."

"And we've got our own business," Alicia added proudly.

"It's incredible." Carmen looked a little dumbfounded. "I feel so lucky."

Jamie disagreed. "Not me," she told her friends. "Luck had nothing to do with it. We've worked really hard to be this successful."

Alicia looked at her friend admiringly. As confident as she felt herself to be, Jamie was even more so. Part of the fun of being Jamie's friend was trying to channel some of her bravado.

"Speaking of successful, I received a very interesting e-mail yesterday." Alicia pointed to her iPad.

"Let me guess," Jamie said. "Someone wants us to plan their *quince*."

Alicia took a seat at the high-topped table and fanned her drink to cool it off. She took a packet of sugar out of her army-navy-style hobo purse.

Carmen laughed. "You know who else keeps sugar in her purse? My seventy-year-old grandmother from Argentina."

Alicia smiled and said, "That's because your *abuela* is very, very wise. Don't hate, appreciate."

Jamie pointed to the iPad and said, "So, the next client—who is it?"

They had planned *quinces* for girls from every imaginable background—from *Boricuas* to *Baranquilleras*. They had planned a space-themed *quince*, a *quince* on a yacht, and even a goth Latina *quince* on a cattle ranch in Texas. And they did their best to throw unforgettable parties—regardless of the client's budget. Big paychecks were nice, but they all agreed that their "under a thousand" *quinces* were some of the best parties they'd ever thrown.

"It's quite mysterious, actually," Alicia said. "Check this out." And she showed them the e-mail.

Dear Amigas Inc.,

It is with great delight that I write you on behalf of my client, a young woman of some renown—who, along with her parents, would like to enlist your services to plan what we hope will be a simply extraordinary *quince*.

The date we have in mind is Saturday, December 15. It is necessary to maintain a mystery about this event, at my client's request.

If you are available to take on this assignment, then all details will be managed via e-mail by me, the client's personal secretary.

Cordialmente,
Julia Centavo

Jamie looked at the dozens of students making their way across the campus. "Clearly, this is a joke," she remarked. "Someone is just having a laugh."

Alicia shook her head. "That was my first thought, too. Which is why I wrote back right away."

She read them her reply.

Dear Miss Centavo,

We appreciate your interest. But we are busy students and entrepreneurs. We simply don't have the time to pursue a "mystery *quince*."

Sinceramente,
Alicia Cruz

"Okay, so the prank is dealt with. Conversation over, right?" said Carmen.

Alicia shook her head, tapped her iPad, and pulled up another e-mail.

Dear Ms. Cruz,

Of course, your time is valuable. And as such, and in consideration of the logistical complications of keeping this client's identity a secret, we'd like to offer you a two hundred dollar signing bonus, which we have taken the liberty of wiring to your account.

Hasta pronto,
Julia Centavo

"This is starting to freak me out a little bit," Carmen said. "Doesn't it all seem a little Da Vinci Code to you?"

"Forget about conspiracy fiction," Jamie jumped in, cutting to the chase. "First, check our account to see if the money is there."

Alicia pulled up their bank's home page and tapped in the user name and password. She took a deep breath, then turned the screen so her friends could see.

"Two hundred dollars. Deposited at nine this morning," Alicia noted.

"Who's the deposit from?" Carmen asked.

Alicia pulled up the details of the deposit and read: "SAP LLC."

"What's that?" Carmen wondered out loud.

"Who cares?" Jamie said. "Their money is good, I'm in."

"I don't know," Carmen countered. "I like to know who I'm working for. It could be someone shady."

Alicia nodded. "I agree; let's do some investigating. I'm going to try to find out who Julia Centavo is. Carmen, why don't you look into this SAP LLC? Jamie, can you do some online research on all the celebrities who might be celebrating *quinces* in Miami over the next six to eight months?"

"I'm on it, Lici," Carmen said as she gathered her books.

"Me, too," Jamie added, "but right now I've got to get to world history."

Alicia looked at her watch, "I've got two minutes to get all the way over to the Hillman Arts Building. I've got to book."

"I've got sculpting in that building; I'll walk with you," Carmen offered.

Alicia and Carmen gave Jamie a quick hug, then headed together toward their classes. As they parted ways at the studio, where Alicia was about to be late for her black-and-white photography class, Carmen smiled and said, "A mystery *quince; fíjate.* Never a dull moment, huh?"

CHAPTER 3

THAT NIGHT, the girls met at Señora Eng's, a restaurant decorated in a kitschy blend of 1920s Shanghai and 1950s Havana styles. The popular South Beach hangout served the yummiest Cuban Chinese food in town and was always packed. The owner, Fiona Eng, had owned a small catering company before opening her hotter-than-hot dining spot. And the partners of Amigas Inc., with their dedicated noses for talent, had hired her to cater several *quinces* when she was first starting out. So, in spite of the fact that this was hardly the usual high school hang, there was always a table at Señora Eng's for Alicia, Jamie, and Carmen.

It was just six when the girls sat down at their favorite table in the corner, beneath a giant framed photograph of the silver-screen star Anna May Wong.

One of the things the *amigas* loved about Señora Eng's was the mix of Miami residents that the restaurant drew. Their waiter, Caleb, was no exception to Fiona's rule of diversity. He was Iranian, with pale brown skin, jet black hair, and a pitch-perfect British accent. He smiled at the girls and said, "I won't bother bringing you menus, since I know exactly what you want: two orders of Havana Dim Sum for the table and watermelon *agua fresca* all around. Am I correct?"

Jamie smiled and said flirtatiously, "You are absolutely correct."

At that moment, Maxo and Gaz approached the table.

"Is that how you three behave when we're not around?" Gaz asked playfully.

"Yeah," Maxo added. "Flirting shamelessly with the waiters?"

Gaz was Puerto Rican. Tall, with striking brown eyes and adorably, perpetually tousled hair, he looked like a male model. Maxo was Haitian American with a playful closemouthed smile and a mischievous air. He looked like a Caribbean version of the young Bill Gates.

Alicia stood up and kissed Gaz on the lips; his kiss tasted sweet, like the Now and Later candies she knew he kept in the car. She always kidded him that one day he'd have no teeth because he ate so much sweet stuff. "This is a nice surprise," she said when they pulled apart. She hadn't expected to see him that night.

Carmen hugged Maxo and whispered in his ear, "Stalking me, *querido*?"

"We were just planning to get together to do some work on Gaz's van when we realized we don't have to get all sweaty, eat cold pizza, and watch SportsCenter. Hey, we have girlfriends." Maxo grinned and slid into the booth next to Carmen.

"And since you are such creatures of habit, we figured you'd be here," Gaz added.

"And if you weren't here, we figured we'd drop your name, get a table, and have a delicious dinner. Win-win," Maxo explained.

Caleb soon returned with the food, and once Alicia had ordered a few more items, to feed the extra mouths at the table—Chinese-style fried chicken, white rice, and black beans—they got down to the business at hand.

"I'm actually glad you guys are here. You can help us figure out this kind-of bizarre client we have." Alicia filled them in on the e-mail and the two hundred dollars that had shown up in the Amigas Inc. account.

"Let me e-mail this Julia Centavo and doubt her existence," Maxo joked. "Maybe she'll send me a bundle of money, too."

"I'm down with that," Gaz joined in. Then more seriously, he asked, "What have you learned?"

Carmen took a bite of *chicharones* and said, "Well, I spoke to my dad's attorney. He deals with a lot of international companies. He said SAP LLC appears to be legit. It's connected to a sporting goods manufacturer based in Mexico City."

Alicia nodded. "My mom looked into it, too. She said there's no liens or actions filed against SAP in the state of Florida."

"So, the company is good?" Jamie asked.

"As far as we can tell," Alicia replied, a little nervously. "But I couldn't find anything on a Julia Centavo connected to SAP LLC."

"Not a Facebook page or anything?" Jamie asked.

"Nada," Alicia sighed.

Gaz laughed. "So what? She's a secretary to some rich family. She's probably really old."

Alicia wasn't convinced. "Okay. But it bothers me to have all the *quince* details determined by the opinions of some anonymous and possibly out-of-touch old lady."

Carmen had been holding hands with Maxo under the table. As usual, she didn't look worried. "But she's just acting as the intermediary for *Quince* Girl X."

Alicia nodded.

Gaz said, "The real question is: who is your mystery girl?"

Jamie tossed her hair and pulled her iPad out of the bag. "I'm glad you asked, Gaz. I spent the whole afternoon doing research, and I've come up with some interesting possibilities. SAP is an accounting firm. Neither of the two principals of the corporation have daughters that are the right age, but their client list is huge. They handle financial matters for over two hundred and fifty corporations and high-wealth individuals. To protect their clients' privacy, they don't list their names on their Web site, so I've taken another tack. Take a look."

She held the iPad up and scrolled through a series of photos of Latina socialites. The last picture to appear on the slide show was of a beautiful girl with a heart-shaped face and long dark curly hair, walking the red carpet at a movie premiere.

"Exhibit A: Nessa Nadal, daughter of star baseball player Manny Nadal."

"She's not unattractive," Gaz said.

Alicia bopped him with her napkin. "What's that supposed to mean?" She wasn't exactly the jealous type, but it *was* senior year, and, like many girls whose boyfriends were about to head off to different colleges, she found herself hanging on a little tighter than usual.

"Nothing, nothing," Gaz replied. "I mean, if there was a picture of you in a hot dress with your makeup all done up, I'd react exactly the same."

Maxo interrupted him. "Let it go, man, let it go."

"A guy can't even explain himself. . . ." Gaz grumbled.

Pointing to the picture, Alicia continued, "Let's focus. Try to be helpful, guys."

"Okay," Gaz said, "here's a bit of trivia. Manny Nadal's daughter is having her *quince* on Christmas Eve. I know, because the manager of the Gap where I work got invited to it, and that's all he talks about. So she's out."

"Good detective work," Carmen noted.

"Well done," Alicia said, kissing her *novio* on the forehead.

Jamie tapped the next image on the iPad. It was of a gorgeous model in a swimsuit on a beach.

"Boys, any comments?"

Gaz shook his head. "None. I've only got eyes for this girl." He squeezed Alicia.

Maxo winked at Carmen, who reached for his hand.

"Exhibit B: Maritza Callas, the hot new Brazilian supermodel. She turns fifteen on December first, so the December fifteenth timing works."

"That girl is fourteen?" Carmen asked incredulously. "What the heck are they putting in the rice and beans down there?"

Jamie shrugged. "I have no idea."

Alicia shook her head, "I dunno. Models throw parties all the time. I don't get the top secret espionage route for a model. They usually love to have their photos snapped by the paparazzi."

"I kinda agree," Jamie said. "Let's move on."

She brought up an image of a pretty blond woman and her look-alike teenage daughter.

"My only other guess is this *chica*, Scarlett Rodriguez, daughter of the hot talk-show host Bianca Rodriguez, whose show *Bye-Bye, Papi* has some people calling her the new Oprah."

Carmen laughed. "No way. Bianca Rodriguez pries secrets out of people for a living. No way is that woman going on the hush-hush about her daughter's *quinceañera*."

· Everybody at the table laughed.

"Maybe you guys are thinking in the wrong direction," Maxo suggested. "You're thinking about

Hollywood celebrities, but what about other well-known people who keep secrets for a living?"

The members of Amigas Inc. all exchanged looks.

"Are you thinking what I'm thinking?" Alicia asked her friends.

"About a certain highly ranked politician who is originally from Miami?" Carmen played along.

"Yesenia Ortega, the American ambassador to Mexico. I'm googling her daughter Carmela now. . . ." Jamie held up the computer. "Carmela Ortega turns fifteen on . . . wait for it . . . December seventeenth."

"I believe we have a winner, ladies and gentlemen," Carmen said, clapping.

Alicia sat back in her chair, stunned. "Wow, I can't believe it. We've been asked to throw a *quince* for one of the most high-profile Latinas in the country," she whispered.

"For the *daughter* of one of the most high-profile Latinas in the country, to be exact," Jamie pointed out.

"Same diff," Alicia replied.

Jamie nodded. "Absolutely same diff." The magnitude of the situation hit Alicia, then Jamie, then Carmen like a wave.

"Do you think there'll be Secret Service men?" Carmen asked, her eyes wide.

Maxo nodded. "If it's Carmela Ortega, there'll be Secret Service men and women. Let's not be sexist."

"There'll probably be royalty from other countries . . . princes and princesses," Alicia said softly.

"We've got to come up with a really good theme," Carmen added.

"One that represents *America*," Jamie said emphatically.

"No," Alicia said. "One that perfectly represents this girl."

"Whom you've never met," Gaz pointed out.

"And won't meet till the day of the event," Maxo said. "Tall order."

"Yeah," Gaz said, enfolding Alicia in a hug and kissing her gently on the cheek. "I'd wish you good luck, but honestly, Lici, you're so talented, luck won't have anything to do with it."

CHAPTER 4

THE NEXT MORNING, Alicia walked into the kitchen to find Maribelle, the cook, making a feast: chocolate-chip waffles, bacon, banana bread with pecan-and-brown-sugar glaze, fruit salad, and fresh papaya smoothies. Maribelle had been with the Cruz family since Alicia was a baby and was less an employee and more a bonus *abuela*.

"Whoa, whoa, who's coming to breakfast?" Alicia asked as she surveyed the counters and the ever so slightly frazzled Maribelle. It had been only three weeks since Alicia's older brother, Alex, had gone off to college, but Maribelle, more than Alicia's parents, even, seemed to be experiencing a bad case of empty-nest syndrome. She still set the table for four at dinnertime, still picked up a six-pack of coconut water every time she went grocery-shopping, even though the unopened cartons now crowded the second shelf of the pantry.

Alicia walked over to Maribelle and gave her a hug. "Alex is at college. Who are you cooking for?"

Maribelle wagged her finger and said, "I'm not senile yet! I know Alex is at college. I light a candle for him at church every week. But this breakfast is for you, *niña*. Isn't today the big college-fair day?"

Alicia gulped. In all the excitement over Carmela Ortega's *quinceañera*, she'd completely forgotten that today was the day when college reps from around the country descended on C. G. High. The reps were there, allegedly, to distribute information and to give students a flesh-and-blood representation of their respective schools. But everybody knew that college day was the academic equivalent of a record company label coming to see your band—the reps were there scouting talent, and a good meeting could do more for your chances of getting into your dream school than even the most pristine application or gushing recommendation.

Alicia looked down at her outfit. The black silk romper with cuffed shorts, the patterned tights and T-strap heels had been perfectly fine for a regular Tuesday. But this wasn't a regular Tuesday. "I'd better change," she mumbled.

In the hallway, she bumped into her mother, who looked shocked to see her in glittery tights. "You're not wearing those for college day, are you?"

Alicia fought the temptation to roll her eyes. "Nope, Mom, I'm changing."

Her father was just coming out of the bathroom and caught a glimpse of her outfit. "Shorts, Lici?" he said.

Alicia grimaced, "No, *Papi*, I'm changing."

Then, just in case any of her friends might have been as absentminded as she was, she sent a text to her whole crew: *Heads up, people. College day. Dress to Impress.*

Right away, her phone started buzzing.

Jamie wrote back: *Thanks for looking out for us, Lici. Changing now.*

Carmen texted: *I was asleep. Audrey Hepburn marathon on AMC last night. Gracias for the wake-up call.*

Maxo wrote: *Breaking out my special occasion Converses.*

And Gaz sent a picture of himself wearing a tie and a note that said: *GQ enough 4U?*

Alicia laughed and quickly changed into one of her mother's hand-me-downs, a respectable, but fun, cherry red wrap dress. She added a pair of black tights, a pair of black leather boots, and her lucky charm: a silver letter *A* on a chain, which her parents had gotten her for Christmas the year before.

Returning to the kitchen, she helped herself to a chocolate-chip waffle, heaped a pile of strawberries on it, and covered the whole concoction with whipped cream. She was about to fold the waffle in half to eat as a sandwich at the bus stop when her mother said, "Whoa, *chica*, slow down. I'll drive you to school. Sit down and eat like a sane person."

Relieved, Alicia took a seat at the dining table with her parents.

"You look very nice, Lici," her father commented, a twinkle in his eyes. He was the city's deputy mayor; he'd left a thriving law practice for public service. Alicia knew that it was from her father that she had gotten her gift for gab and the desire to help people, or as Gaz jokingly called it, her buttinsky gene.

Alicia's mom was a judge, and she had the take-charge mentality that was needed in order to preside over the largest district court in Miami. Alicia wasn't sure if she'd inherited her mother's gift for organization or if it had just been drilled into her since the age of six, but having to buy her own school supplies and submit to weekly inspections of her pencil box, her backpack, and her lunch box, she, like her brother, Alex, had learned how to make lists and budgets, and to maintain their personal belongings with neatness and precision.

It was certainly from her mother that Alicia had inherited her love of style. Every year, over the Christmas holiday, she and her mom picked a night to stay up late and watch their favorite movie, *Celestial Clockwork*. And in the scene where Ariel D. sings "*La ropa, la ropa, la ropa*" (clothes, clothes, clothes), they always got up to sing along. A few years back, *Miami* magazine had even named her mother on its list of best-dressed Floridians, praising her for wearing suits made by up-and-coming local South Beach designers.

Alicia's parents had met at Harvard Law School, and the question of whether she would follow in their footsteps was always in the air. Her parents never pushed, they merely suggested. But for an overachiever like Alicia, the difference between a push and a suggestion was not always so easily discerned. Alicia's brother had cleverly sidestepped the issue by getting into a superprestigious engineering program at McGill University in Montreal, which her parents proudly told friends was the Harvard of the North.

"So, remind me of the schools that you're meeting with today," her father asked, helping himself to another slice of banana bread.

"Columbia, Brown, Penn, Yale, and Harvard," Alicia replied.

"*Hmmm*, Harvard. I think I've heard of that school."

Alicia smiled. Dad humor—never subtle, always cheery. She wondered if it were part of the deal before a dad could bring his child home from the hospital: if he had to promise never to tell a joke that was actually funny.

Her mother, as usual, was much more businesslike. "Do we know the name of the Harvard rep who's visiting the school today?"

Alicia shook her head.

Her father smiled. "Gosh, I hope it's not my freshman-year roommate, David Lawrence. I still owe that guy five dollars."

Alicia grinned at her father. "Don't quit your day job, Dad. Stand-up's not your thing. On an entirely different subject, we've figured out who our mystery *quince* is."

Her parents exchanged glances, which Alicia took to mean that they wanted to talk college, not *quinces*.

"Come on, you guys. Guess," she pleaded.

"Is she famous?" her mother asked.

"Does she go to your school?" her father wondered.

"Oh, you're both hopeless," Alicia said. "It's Carmela Ortega."

Her parents looked at each other blankly.

"Daughter of Yesenia Ortega, the US ambassador to Mexico," Alicia said, beaming. "Pretty impressive, don't you think?"

"Wow, that is impressive," her father said. "And do your friends agree?"

Alicia nodded, "Absolutely. It all fits. She turns fifteen on December seventeenth, two days after the requested party day. She's originally from Miami. And she has to keep any event a secret—it's a matter of national security. This *quince* is going to be swarming with Secret Service men—and women. There're Secret Service women, too."

Her dad let out a little laugh.

"What?" Alicia asked.

"Secret Service women?" he said. "That's funny. I mean, in my day, we said women could do anything, but nobody really believed it. We just said it so they wouldn't whomp us over the heads with their pocketbooks."

Alicia looked at her mother. "Tell me he's kidding, right?"

Marisol stood up. "Of course he's kidding. Now, let me drive you to school before we're both late."

"Next thing you know, you're going to tell me women can play pro basketball and run for president." Her father winked at Alicia.

"I love you, Dad," she said, kissing him on the forehead.

Her father hugged her. "You know we're proud, regardless of where you go to school." Then he took five dollars out of his wallet. "But just in case, take this, in case you happen to run into that Lawrence guy from Harvard."

CHAPTER 5

DOZENS OF SENIORS gathered nervously in front of the giant bulletin board outside the principal's office. The sign said: C. G. HIGH COLLEGE FAIR, and beneath it was a printout of every student's name and his or her assignment. Alicia tried to get close enough to see her name and schedule, but the students in front of her blocked her view. Her crew was nowhere in sight, so she assumed that they had either already been to the board or were running later than she was.

"*Hola*, Alicia!"

She turned to see Patricia Reinoso, one of C. G. High's star basketball players. Amigas Inc. had planned a double *quince* for Patricia and her cousin Carolina the year before, and they'd all ended up becoming good friends.

Patricia kissed Alicia on both cheeks and gestured to the crowd. "It doesn't happen often, but this is one of those days when I'm happy to be a junior, not a senior."

"Enjoy it while it lasts," Alicia said, feeling all of a sudden much older than her seventeen years.

Of course, what with running Amigas Inc., spending time with Gaz, and maintaining a 4.0 GPA, Alicia's junior year had seemed a marathon of deadlines and obligations. But now, with a little distance, she could see that being a junior had been particularly sweet. She had been an upperclassman, with none of the anxiety or fears that accompanied freshman or even sophomore year. At the time, the prospect of choosing a college—the institution that would define her grown-up life and career—was a million miles away. This year, she had all the cachet of being a senior, but all of the anxiety, too. And of course, next year, she'd be a freshman all over again. Unless fate intervened, she wouldn't be going to the same college or even living in the same city as Jamie and Carmen, or even her sweetheart, Gaz.

"Promise me you'll go to lots of parties," Alicia told Patricia. "School dances, school trips—before you know it, it will all be over."

Patricia looked ever so slightly worried. "Okay, Lici, if you say so."

"Hey, relax a little, drama queen," Jamie said, tapping

Alicia on the shoulder. "It's the end of high school, not *The End of the Affair*."

The End of the Affair was one of Alicia's favorite old movies, and she had made all of her friends sit through at least two screenings of it—especially since they inevitably fell asleep during the first one.

"Who's having an affair?" Carmen asked, joining them. She held a sheet of paper that had her schedule typed out on it.

"No one," Alicia said. "How'd you get your appointments typed out all nice and neat?"

Carmen smiled, "I went to see my adviser, Ms. Ingber."

"Oooh, good thinking," Jamie said. "It's like a roller derby trying to get to that board. People are throwing elbows, jabbing you with pens and whatnot."

Maxo and Gaz walked over, each with pristine copies of their schedules.

"You guys went to see your advisers, too?" Alicia asked. "That's where I'm heading."

Maxo shook his head, "Too late; you missed the window. The trick was to get in before the list went up. Now the advisers' offices are filled with people complaining."

"Complaining about what?" Jamie asked.

"Not every student got their first pick. It all depended on which reps showed up and how many time slots they had."

Gaz held up his schedule. "MIT wasn't on my list. I don't have the grades or the money. But apparently there're a lot of musicians among the geek ranks, and the rep wants to meet me."

"That's pretty impressive, babe, being singled out by MIT," said Alicia. She was proud of him—cute, talented, and nice. Gaz was the boyfriend trifecta.

Turning to Jamie, she said, "The crowd's thinning; let's check out our schedules."

"Can we meet later for dinner?" Gaz asked.

"Sure. Señora Eng's?" Alicia asked.

"Where else?" Gaz kissed her sweetly on the cheek.

"*Buena suerte*, peeps!" Alicia said, waving to Gaz, Carmen, and Maxo as they walked away. She stood next to Jamie at the nearly empty board. "Okay, what have we got?" she asked.

"You've got: Brown at ten fifteen, Harvard at eleven, Yale at eleven thirty, Columbia at twelve, and Penn at twelve thirty," Jamie replied.

"Those were all my picks," Alicia noted as she scribbled them down. "What have you got?"

Jamie read off the list: "Columbia at ten thirty,

Cooper Union at ten forty-five, Brown and RISD at eleven thirty, Savannah College of Design at twelve, and NYU at twelve thirty."

"This is nuts," Alicia said, staring at her schedule. "It's like speed dating."

"Kind of," Jamie said. "Except your entire future depends on it."

Alicia turned to give her friend a hug, *"Buena suerte, chica."*

Jamie smiled. "Right back atcha."

Alicia's first appointment was in the gym. She found the Brown University rep and took a seat at the small table across from the woman.

"Hi, I'm Alicia," she said, reaching to shake the woman's hand.

The rep, Melinda Davies, was younger than Alicia had expected. She was in her twenties, African American, and dressed in a khaki shift and blazer.

"So, Alicia," Melinda began, "how would you describe yourself in one word?"

Alicia panicked. She was good at talking to adults. She had the ability to convince parents to entrust hundreds, even thousands of dollars to a business run by teenagers who weren't old enough to vote. But somehow this question stumped her.

Without any idea of what the right answer was, she told the Brown rep that if she had had to describe herself in one word, she would have had to say *lucky*.

Melinda Davies raised an eyebrow and scribbled something down on her pad. "Tell me what you mean by that," she said.

"I feel really fortunate that my grandparents came to this country with nothing but the clothes on their backs, and yet through hard work they were able to send my parents to school, and my parents have done so well. My mom is a kick-butt lawyer, and my dad . . ."

Ms. Davies cut her off: "So, do you feel like you've been coasting on your family's success?"

Alicia turned red. "Not at all. My friends and I have our own business—Amigas Inc."

Ms. Davies looked down at her notes. "It's a party-planning business?"

Alicia tried not to sound defensive. "Oh, no, it's more than a party-planning business. A *quinceañera* is a major rite of passage in the life of any Latina—it's a way to honor your culture, your heritage, your community."

The Brown rep seemed pleased with the answer and asked, "So, did this business start with your own *quinceañera*?"

Alicia shook her head. "I actually didn't have one. I took a trip instead."

Ms. Davies looked at her watch and said, "Well, our time is almost up. Anything I can tell you about Brown?"

Flustered, Alicia asked, "Is it true that you don't have any grades?"

Ms. Davies looked displeased. "Yes, that is true. And if your GPA is the only way you know to measure success, then Brown is probably not the place for you."

The rep stood up and extended her hand, and Alicia shook it. "Nice meeting you, Alicia," she said.

Alicia smiled back, but it was all she could do to keep from saying, *Oh, yeah? Well, it kinda sucked meeting you.*

Her next appointment—with Harvard—was in the auditorium. In the hallway, she passed a glowing Carmen.

"The rep from FIT spent the whole time oohing and aahing over my portfolio," Carmen gushed. "How's it going for you?"

Alicia was desperate to keep up appearances, mostly because she'd never had any academic disappointments to share. She was Alicia "Straight A" Cruz. She had struggled on the boy front, at least before she got together with Gaz. Her Spanish-language skills were fair to middling at best. But she had never struggled at school—yet part of what worried her was that college would require abilities she didn't have.

Alicia gave Carmen a thumbs-up and said, "It's all good in the C.G. hood."

Walking into the auditorium, she thought maybe she could borrow a page from Carmen's book. She didn't have a portfolio like Carmen's for her designs, but she did have a gallery of the *quinces* she'd planned. And she needed all the help she could get. She *couldn't* blow this one.

Serena Shih, the Harvard rep, was a petite Korean American in her thirties with what Alicia thought of as New York hair—the kind of crisp New York bob that looked as if it had been cut in one easy go, but which actually involved elaborate layering to give it its perfect fullness and swing.

Ms. Shih, too, asked Alicia the dreaded describe-yourself-in-one-word question, but this time, instead of panicking, Alicia said, "I'd use two words: *entrepreneurial* and *cultural*." Then she took out her iPad and told Ms. Shih all about Amigas Inc.—how she herself had never had a *quince*, because she had thought it was an expensive, over-the-top party thrown by girls who simply longed to spend one night in a big, poufy dress.

"The thing is that a *quince* is about so much more than the dress," Alicia went on. "Along with my best friends, who are also my business partners, we help girls plan celebrations that exemplify who they are and who they want to be as Latinas today."

Ms. Shih smiled, "I have to tell you, I'm very impressed. I see a lot of businesses and foundations allegedly run by teenagers, but the parents are often doing all the work. This is something you truly own."

"It is," Alicia said proudly.

"Have you heard of the two plus two program at Harvard?"

Alicia shook her head.

"It's a program we developed a few years ago to encourage liberal arts undergraduates to pursue MBAs. Companies like Google and McKinsey don't want straight engineers and numbers crunchers. They want creative managers—people like you."

Ms. Shih explained that if Alicia came to Harvard, she could apply for the two plus two program at the end of her junior year. She handed Alicia her card. "I work here in Miami. This meeting schedule doesn't give me enough time to talk about something this important with a candidate as promising as you. Call my office, and we'll meet for coffee one day after school."

Alicia practically floated toward the next meeting. The two interviews she'd had couldn't have been more different. It was strange to do so poorly, then so well. She hadn't changed in the half hour between the two interviews. But what was really trippy was how perfect the two plus two program at Harvard sounded to her. Alicia went to the other meetings and did her iPad presentations, but really all she could think of was Harvard, Harvard, Harvard.

She ran to the cafeteria to grab a sandwich before her afternoon class and was surprised to see Carmen and Jamie there, leisurely eating. She knew they both had one o'clock classes, too.

"Aren't you guys worried about being late for class?" Alicia asked as she took a big bite of her tuna sandwich.

"It's college day," Carmen explained, holding up a late pass. "You can get a pass from your adviser."

"That works," Alicia said. "In that case, I'm going to get some fro yo."

She returned to the table with a bowl of chocolate soft-serve and laughed at the worn-out expressions on her friends' faces. "Do I look as beat up as you two do?"

"No, and it's annoying," Jamie said, resting her head on the cafeteria table.

"Describe yourself in one word," Carmen said to Jamie.

"Exhausted," Jamie said.

"Now, somebody, ask me," Carmen said.

Alicia smiled, happy to discover that she wasn't the only one who'd found the question annoying.

"Describe yourself in one word, Carmen," Alicia said.

"Confused," Carmen replied.

The bell rang for the next class, and Jamie said, "Let's all have dinner tonight."

"Can't," Alicia replied. "I have a date with Gaz."

Jamie shook her head. "No way. It's college day, and I need my *chicas*. Pass me your phone."

Alicia handed Jamie her cell.

Jamie dialed a stored number and winked at Alicia. "Hello?" she said.

Gaz must have said something sweet on the other end of the line, because Jamie laughed out loud. "Does your girlfriend know you call me *baby*?

"Look, Gazissimo," Jamie continued. "That little speed round of college *Jeopardy* just about kicked my butt. And sadly, Dash, my go-to source for TLC is hitting the books at Duke and not available, so I'm inviting myself on your date tonight. Does that work for you?" She smiled into the phone. "Thanks. You're a good guy, Gaz. Can Carmen and Maxo come, too?" She paused. "*Excelente, mi jefe.* We'll see you for dinner 'round six."

Jamie returned the phone to Alicia. "See you tonight, *amigas.* Stay strong."

Alicia walked down to the guidance counselor's office and knocked on the door of her adviser, Mr. Stevens. She hardly ever visited his office. In all honesty, she thought of herself as a dispenser of good advice, not someone who needed it.

"Hey, Mr. Stevens, I got caught up in college day, and I heard you could give me a late pass for my next class."

"Sure, sure," Mr. Stevens said. He was tall, blond, and tanned, with the easy disposition of a man who started every day surfing at the beach, which he did. He also taught AP macroeconomics, which was a class that landed squarely on Alicia's Always Say Never list.

"College day. How'd it go?" Mr. Stevens asked genially. "Take a seat. Let me pull your file; we'll hang."

"It's okay, Mr. Stevens, I'll just take the late pass and go," Alicia replied.

"And miss out on the opportunity to chill with me?" he said. "What do you have now? Classics? Or, as I like to call it, Literature Written by Dead People 101? You're a senior; we've got to talk about your future."

Alicia sighed and took a seat. Mr. Stevens was a good teacher and a nice enough guy, but she found that his efforts to relate to his students by putting himself on what he considered their level a little overdone and condescending.

"So, how'd it go? Who rocked your world today?"

It was such a funny question. If Alicia were to answer honestly—and she didn't see any point in lying—Serena Shih from Harvard was hands down the most exciting rep. So she told Mr. Stevens all about her iPad demo and Serena and Harvard's two plus two MBA program.

"That's crazy, man," Mr. Stevens observed. "It's like you were meant for each other."

"And you know the best part of it all? She never mentioned my parents or the fact that Harvard has to take me because I'm a legacy."

"That's cool. Shows she's got character," her counselor said. He'd obviously grown either bored or comfortable, because he had stopped reading her file and begun tossing a Nerf football back and forth with her. "So, what's the problem?"

Alicia missed catching the ball; she picked it up from the floor. How did he know? She hadn't even admitted it to herself yet, but she *was* worried about something. "The problem is that I'm a legacy. Both of my parents went to Harvard. They *have* to take me."

Mr. Stevens put the ball down and looked at her with that grown-up "Are you doing drugs/smoking cigarettes/breaking the law?" stare. He said, "It's Harvard, Alicia. They don't *have* to do anything but sit on a pile of money and drop their *R*'s."

Alicia shook her head, "You don't understand. I'm a type A, second-generation, high-achieving Latina. My grandparents went against the grain by coming to this country. My parents overcame the odds and went to Harvard. Even though I grew up in cushy Coral Gables, do you think my parents or the Harvard admissions office aren't going to say, 'Of course, she belongs at Harvard, too'?"

Mr. Stevens sighed. "Alicia, you're a seventeen-year-old whiz entrepreneur. You've found this incredible niche where you make money by helping young women connect to a deeply meaningful cultural tradition. You are already one of a kind. Don't choose a college based upon the need to be the same as, different from, or better than your parents. Choose the place where *you* want to go."

The bell rang, and Alicia rose from her chair. "Looks like I missed my Literature Written by Dead People class."

Mr. Stevens said, "Don't worry, I'll let Mrs. Suber know. Let's keep talking, Alicia. I'm here to help you figure this stuff out."

She smiled. It was actually as satisfying to receive advice as it was to dish it out. She stood at the door and then turned. "So, where'd you go to college, Mr. Stevens?"

He pointed to his board. "UC Santa Barbara. Majored in surfing, minored in economics. Now I teach in Miami and get to catch the waves every day of the week. I'm living my dream, Alicia. Hope you get to live yours."

CHAPTER 6

THAT NIGHT, Alicia arrived at the restaurant to find Gaz, Maxo, Carmen, and Jamie already seated. She squeezed in next to Gaz, who said, "Describe yourself in one word."

Alicia groaned. "Are we still playing that game?"

Gaz laughed. "Are you kidding? This game rocks. It's both misery-inducing and inherently interesting."

"Okay, then," Alicia said. "You first. What did you say?"

"I said I was mysterious," Gaz replied.

Jamie and Alicia burst out laughing.

Carmen put her hand over her mouth to stifle a giggle. "He's kidding, right?"

Maxo nudged Gaz and added, "Well, I said I was a genius."

"Okay, so I'm a tad gullible. Now I know you're both kidding," Carmen said.

As they passed around a bamboo tray of steamed dumplings, Alicia asked, "I don't get it, Maxo. If you're deferring school for a year to volunteer in Haiti, why are you even putting yourself through this gruesome process?"

Maxo popped a dumpling in his mouth and put a finger up to indicate that he was still chewing. Then he said, "Because, in order to defer college a year, you actually have to be accepted and enrolled in a school. So, I'm pretty much in the same boat as the rest of you—dream school, safety school, and eight tedious applications in between."

"The thing I don't get," Carmen said, "is why do we have to apply to so many schools? In my mom's day, you'd apply to four or five. Now, any sane person applies to at least ten. I'm seriously thinking about doing early decision to Parsons. No muss, no fuss. FIT and Parsons have been the two schools I've always wanted to go to, and I had a great meeting with the rep from Parsons today. She convinced me that I'd be a perfect fit."

Alicia always admired Carmen's steadiness. Her friend had wanted to be a fashion designer since she was six. And she had wanted to go to a college specializing in art and design since seventh grade, when she had asked her parents for the season one DVD boxed set of *Project Runway* for Christmas and proceeded to watch all twelve episodes back to back while the rest of her family slept.

"To Carmen and Parsons," Alicia toasted, raising a glass of *agua fresca* to toast her friend. "And to the rest of us—may we figure it out."

Gaz turned to Jamie. "What about you, J.? You've been talking NYU, Columbia, and get me out of hot Miami and back to *Nueva* York ever since I met you. What are you thinking?"

Jamie smiled and took a bite of her pork chop with black bean sauce. "I know I've been talking about the East Coast and New York forever . . . and maybe I was a little pushy about the greatest city in the world. But college is all about new experiences, right? After I met with the guy from NYU, I stopped by to talk to the rep from Stanford."

Alicia almost spit out her *pollo a la brasa.* "Stanford? As in, California?"

Jamie got that fierce don't-mess-with-the-Bronx-bombshell look that she broke out from time to time. "Why, yes, Stanford. Did I stutter?"

Gaz whistled. "California! What's up with that?"

Jamie blushed. "Well, Dash is thinking about transferring to Stanford. . . ."

Before Alicia could stop herself, she blurted out, "But Jamie, you can't choose a college based on where your boyfriend goes."

Jamie glared at her, and Alicia felt as if they'd time-warped back to the beginning of their friendship, when Jamie was always being the hard-core New York girl and Alicia was always saying the wrong thing.

"Alicia, if you would let a person finish . . ." Jamie growled. "I stopped by the Stanford desk just to mention Dash and how he wanted me to visit the school with him over Christmas break. One thing led to another, and it turns out that the rep is a museum curator at an Asian arts museum in San Francisco. I told him about my eBay store and how much I sell to kids in Tokyo and Seoul. He said Stanford has an amazing Far East studies program and all kinds of arts exchanges. I never thought of the customized pimped-out sneakers and handbags I design as art, but he pointed out all the cool fashion-art collaborations over the years, like Malick Sidibé for agnès b. and Murakami for Louis Vuitton. He thought I might find art school too limiting, and that double-majoring in fine art and Asian studies might be more inspiring."

"Wow," Alicia said.

"That's all you have to say? 'Wow'?" Jamie grumbled.

Alicia could tell her friend was mad at her for sure and probably would be for a while. She shook her head. "I mean, *wow*, I'm really impressed."

"We're all impressed," Carmen added brightly, playing the peacemaker and cheerleader. "You'd be amazing at Stanford, Jamie."

"Well, I was sort of surprised in my meetings, too," Gaz piped up. "Berklee College of Music is clearly my first choice. But MIT was kind of impressive, too. They've got mad financial aid, and the music department guy said that a lot of musicians never finish Berklee, because they get a record deal or a part in a Broadway show. He said if I really wanted to spend four years living and breathing music as an art and not the music *business*, I should think about MIT."

Feeling as if words were failing her, Alicia hugged Gaz tight. The purity of his feelings for his music had been one of the first things she'd loved about him.

"So, Maxo," Gaz said, "from what fine institution will you be deferring admission?"

Maxo shrugged. "Ideally, Columbia. Their international studies program is just the best. And hopefully, being in New York, I could intern at the United Nations, begin to explore a career that mixes diplomacy with technology."

Alicia looked around at her friends. They were so smart, so unique. She was lucky they even let her hang with them.

"What about you, Lici?" Carmen asked. "Any of those Ivies looking good?"

This would've been the moment to tell them about Harvard, about the two plus two program and her fears of being another unimaginative legacy candidate. She'd let it all out with Mr. Stevens, and she barely knew him. But something about her own uncertainty and the way Jamie was shooting dirty looks at her while texting on her BlackBerry made Alicia pause.

She shrugged. "I'm really not sure yet."

Gaz, Carmen, and Jamie exchanged glances. Not sure? About her number one college pick? Over-the-top, ultraprepared, I'll Rule High School Today and the World Tomorrow Alicia Cruz? Alicia, who put the *A* in type A? It really didn't seem likely.

Even Maxo, who'd known Alicia for only a few short months, was suspicious. "Well, how did your meetings go?" he asked.

"Hmmm. After meeting with Columbia, Harvard, Yale, Penn, and Brown, if I had to describe myself in one word, I'd say I was *impressed* and *overwhelmed*."

Gaz squeezed Alicia's shoulder. "That's two words, *mi amor*."

Alicia shrugged and picked up the dessert menu. "I'm starving," she said. "Who's up for splitting an order of chocolate and banana wontons?"

"Me," said Carmen.

"Me, too," agreed Jamie, looking up from the text she was sending Dash.

"I'm in," nodded Maxo.

Only Gaz dissented. "No way," he said. "If everybody wants dessert, no way are we splitting one order. We'd better order two. Matter of fact, they're small—let's order three. Maxo and I are growing boys."

As the conversation shifted to dessert, SAT prep classes, and weekend plans, Alicia felt relieved that she had dodged her friends' questions. She could feel her shoulders drop from the tense, up-near-the-ears clinch they'd been in just moments earlier.

That night, when Gaz dropped her off at home, they stayed in the car for a few minutes kissing good-bye again and again.

" 'Night, Gaz," Alicia whispered.

"*Buenas noches*, beautiful," Gaz replied, kissing her even longer.

She smiled and took her hair out of the ponytail it had been in all day.

"So, I'll see you tomorrow?" she asked.

Despite the growing success of Gaz's band and his songwriting deal, he still worked twenty hours a week at the Gap. Gaz's father was deceased, and his mother, Inez, worked as a live-in maid for a wealthy Panamanian family. Having been promoted to assistant manager, he was able to get health-care coverage for his brother and mother.

"Listen, Lici," Gaz murmured, "I love your friends. But we haven't been on a date, a real date, in *forever*. I want to . . . I mean, I need to spend some time alone with you alone, just us."

Alicia nodded. He was, of course, completely right.

"So, what do you have in mind?" she asked playfully.

"Something really nice," he said. "Are you free Saturday night?"

Alicia pretended to think about it. "Hmmm. I dunno. I'll have to check my schedule. . . . Let me call my boyfriend and see if he's working. . . ." Then she started giggling so much she couldn't tease him anymore. "Of course I'm free! I'll always get time freed up for you," she said, kissing him again.

Gaz grinned. "Okay, be sure to dress up. We're

going somewhere fancy," he said, looking excited.

"Um . . ." Alicia said, gesturing toward her vintage dress and suede ankle boots, "basic Amigas Inc. dress code is fabulous. You only have to tell me when you want me to dress *down*."

Gaz laughed, "My bad, my bad. Let's kiss and make up."

He kissed her again, for a very long time—so long that her father came to the door and waved. "I should've turned off my headlights," Gaz grumbled.

He walked Alicia to the front door, where she greeted her father. "Hey, Dad, thanks for staying up to make sure I got home safely."

Then, without waiting for her father to answer, Alicia floated up to her room.

CHAPTER 7

ON SATURDAY NIGHT, Alicia put on her favorite new dress, a one-shoulder number that she'd bought with her earnings from Amigas Inc.

Alicia's mother acted as the girls' accountant. Every three months, she divided the company's earnings into thirds. One third went toward the girls' 529 College Savings Plan funds—money they could use in the not-too-distant future for everything from room and board to textbooks. Another third of the earnings went back into the company, to cover future expenses. And the final third was divided among Jamie, Alicia, and Carmen, to do with as they wished.

Alicia was shocked at how quickly her checks from Amigas Inc. began to double and triple what her allowance had been. Now her parents saved that money for college, and she used her Amigas Inc. earnings to buy everything from dresses to iTunes downloads and books.

She hesitated before choosing the shoes to complete her outfit. All week long she'd been pressing Gaz for clues about their date and all he would say was "fancy and grown-up." Her mind kept flashing back to the ice-cold air-conditioned restaurants in Coconut Grove where her father sometimes met clients. She hoped that Gaz wouldn't waste his hard-earned money on one of those dreadfully expensive, fancy-silver-and-heavy-crystal-goblet eateries.

Gaz rang the doorbell promptly at seven. He was dressed in a khaki sports coat, a crisp white shirt, and a tie. He'd gotten a haircut, and while the lock that hung over his left eye was impossible to tame, he looked sharp and clean-shaven. It was quite a change from his usual ruggedly handsome, casual rocker look.

Alicia whistled. "Wow, you clean up good."

Her mother came to the front door and gave him a warm hug. "Gaz, I'm very impressed. Did the mystery *quince* inspire your mystery date?"

Gaz smiled. "No, Señora Cruz, this was all my own idea."

Her mother crossed her arms in front of her and pretended to look at the couple sternly. "You two aren't going to elope, are you?"

Alicia rolled her eyes. "Mom, so not funny."

As usual, her mother thought being embarrassing was part of her charm. "And no using fake IDs to get on a booze cruise?"

Gaz looked horrified at the suggestion and protested emphatically, "I would *never.*"

Alicia's mother looked satisfied. "Well, how about an ETA for when you'll bring Alicia home, or is that also a mystery?" She winked at Gaz.

"Oh, no," Gaz answered. "We're going somewhere special. So, would twelve thirty work?"

Midnight was Alicia's curfew on the weekend. Her mother had a theory that there was nothing happening after midnight that a nice girl like Alicia or any of her friends needed to partake in.

Gaz asked Alicia to excuse him while he spoke to her mom. Even though she thought he was taking the cloak-and-dagger routine a bit too far, she loved the fact that he still wanted to be imaginative about their dates. She stepped aside and watched, amused, as Gaz whispered something to her mom.

Her mother's smile got wider and wider. Finally, she said, "Nice. Twelve thirty it is. Have fun, kids." She closed the front door, and Gaz and Alicia walked to the car. He held the car door open for her. The moment she clicked shut her seat belt, she turned and kissed him passionately.

"Hey, I like that," Gaz murmured when she was done. "But you haven't even gotten your surprise yet."

"I know," Alicia said. "But that's just to say thank you for being so romantic as to plan the surprise. I know how busy you are with school, your music, and now, college apps. It's sweet, and I appreciate it."

As they drove on to I-95, Gaz played Alicia a new song. "My agent wants to send this song to Sophie Lundquist."

Alicia tried not to let her jaw drop. "*The* Sophie Lundquist?"

Gaz smiled. "Yeah, she's looking to do an album of duets, and he thinks this would be perfect."

Alicia was always impressed by Gaz's music, but ever since the previous spring, when Amigas Inc. had traveled to Austin, and Gaz, who was then one of the company's partners, had attended the South by Southwest conference, she'd seen his commitment to his career move to the next level. The professional musicians that he'd met, the contacts that he'd made, the seminars he'd attended on songwriting and musicianship—had all molded what had been pure talent into something polished and sophisticated. Gaz's late father had been a professional singer in Puerto Rico, not rich or famous, but beloved by many. Alicia found herself wishing, as she often did, that Gaz's father were still alive to see the amazing person his son had become.

The car pulled up in front of the Adrienne Arsht Center on Biscayne Boulevard. The modern white building reminded Alicia of pictures she'd seen of the Sydney Opera House. It was a beautiful arts center, but Alicia felt slightly worried. The last time she'd been there had been with her parents, for a performance of Tchaikovsky's "The Fateful Fourth," which had proven so terminally boring that she'd fallen asleep before the intermission. Her parents hadn't found her sleepiness or her snoring amusing.

"Gaz," she said, putting an arm on his shoulder, "I'll do my best, but classical music is not my thing."

Gaz looked disappointed. "You know how important it is for me to expand my musical repertoire. I thought this evening's tribute to Vienna would be a great adventure for us both. They'll be performing polkas, Strauss waltzes, and operettas—minioperas. And during the intermission, they're serving Wiener schnitzel."

Alicia looked down. She'd broken out her brand-new one-shoulder dress for Wiener schnitzel? Heaven help her. She just couldn't get a break!

She took a deep breath. She always said that living in Miami was all about the cultural mix, even if some of the culture was old and snoozeworthy. And who knows? she thought: she loved dance, so maybe the Strauss waltzes would inspire some sort of *quince* theme for their mystery client. It certainly sounded elegant enough.

Inside the arts center, the room bustled with a mostly Latino crowd. When Gaz handed the usher the two tickets, she directed them to the front of the orchestra. Alicia tried to keep from groaning. Row G. Center. These were amazing seats; the tickets must have cost a fortune! She should have been grateful. Gaz truly was the greatest boyfriend in the world. But as she and her sweet, thoughtful, classical-music-loving boyfriend seated themselves in the middle of the row, all she could think was, *Great, now I'm trapped. I can't even sneak out for a bathroom break! And if I snore, I'm pretty sure the acoustics of this fancy place will ensure that the entire auditorium will hear me. Ugh!*

"You psyched?" Gaz whispered as the lights dimmed.

"Oh, yeah, absolutely," Alicia fibbed, forcing a grin.

As the room grew dark, she heard the sweet music

of a conga drum—the kind of shake-your-hips rhythm that she was fairly confident was not part of any waltz or polka. The curtain went up to reveal an all-star assembly of Latin musicians playing a riveting Cuban *son*. The audience rose like a wave, and everyone began dancing in front of their seats.

Alicia threw her head back and laughed. "You tricked me!" she guffawed as she slid her arm around her boyfriend's waist. "And I am not an easy person to trick."

"Tell me about it," laughed Gaz. "Lucky for you I have a weakness for women who are both smart and unbelievably nosy."

Alicia tilted her head and planted a kiss on his soft lips. "*Gracias, mi amor,*" she whispered.

"You're welcome, Lici," Gaz answered, beaming with pride. "But less talking and more dancing." As he held her hand, Alicia danced and danced. And for a few extraordinary, rhythm-driven hours, she did not think about the SATs or college applications or any of the senior-year responsibilities that had been weighing so heavily on her.

CHAPTER 8

THE NEXT AFTERNOON, the three
partners in Amigas Inc. met at Carmen's house to discuss their mystery *quince*. Carmen lived on the Canals
in Miami, on one of a series of small streets that lined
the water. No cars were allowed, and the houses, while
packed closely together, were beautiful, and looked as
though they had been transplanted from Venice. When
the girls were younger, their favorite thing in the world
had been to take boat rides in the family's little tur-
quoise boat. Now they sat on the patio, watching as
Carmen's younger stepsisters rowed around, laughing
hysterically, with *their* friends.

The contracts for the mystery *quince* were all signed,
and the first payment was in the Amigas account. The
girls sat with their Lucite clipboards, which Alicia's
mom had customized with the hot pink Amigas Inc.
logo. Breaking out the clipboards was always exciting,

but as they sat thumbing through their ten-page events checklists, they were both excited and slightly daunted. Their contact, Julia Centavo, would neither confirm nor deny that their client was, indeed, Carmela Ortega, but the girls were confident nevertheless that they'd cracked their client's secret identity.

"I'm megaexcited about planning Carmela's *quinceañera*," Alicia said. "But I've got to tell you *chicas*, I'm pretty stressed about juggling all that work with everything else on my plate—SAT prep, getting letters of recommendation, requesting transcripts, writing college essays. It's a lot!"

"Who are you telling?" Jamie demanded.

"Ugh, I love Ms. Ingber, but she's making me nuts, the way she has me running and gunning," Carmen said. "What kind of *loca* takes AP Spanish literature when she's applying to art programs?"

All of the Amigas Inc. crew spoke some degree of Spanish, but the truth was that none of them were actually fluent except for Gaz, who'd grown up in Puerto Rico and come to Miami in the fifth grade. Of the three girls, Carmen spoke Spanish the most fluently—partly because of her dad. She had spent so much time on his *telenovela* sets that even when her vocabulary failed her, she could throw in an "¡*Ay, no digas!"* or an energetic *"Sinvergüenza"* that was so convincing that anyone would have taken her for a native speaker.

But that was only part of the story. While Alicia and Jamie had decided to place out of their language requirement in junior year, Carmen had continued, studying literature in the work of writers as diverse as Isabel Allende and Federico García Lorca. It gave her a little thrill to read in Spanish, even if it meant she pored over each page with a pen in one hand and a dictionary in the other. And she loved to see the way the over-the-top romances depicted in her father's films had real cultural roots. To be Latina, she felt every time she opened her current favorite, *Eva Luna*, was to be in love with love.

"So, we're all swamped," Jamie agreed. "What are we going to do? Binky's was the biggest-budget *quince* we ever did. But to do a *quince* that will be attended by luminaries from our nation's government, that's *histori-cal*. We can't mess this up."

Alicia flinched. Even the thought of a misstep with a *quince* gave her the chills. It was because she cared so much about each and every girl's Sweet Fifteen that she sometimes got a little controlling. She hated to admit it, but even though she'd never had a *quince* herself, she'd gone all *quince*-zilla on more than one occasion.

She thought about it for a few moments. "We need help," she said. "But we have a bigger problem. It's the first of October. We're graduating in less than a year, and by the sound of it, none of us are going to school in Miami. Who's going to run Amigas Inc. when we go off to college?"

The girls looked at one another, and the reality that they were going to split up—not right away, but really soon—hit them like a ton of textbooks.

"Maybe I won't get into any schools," Carmen offered wistfully.

"Maybe my financial aid won't come through and I'll have to go to community college," Jamie said.

"And maybe I'll get a two hundred on my SATs," Alicia put in. "But since they give you two hundred points for just signing your name, that doesn't seem likely. No doom and gloom, *chicas*. We don't need to derail our futures so Amigas Inc. can live. What we need is a plan."

Carmen looked appreciatively at her friend. "What we need is successors."

Jamie jumped to her feet. "Let's have a contest! It should be like *The Apprentice*. I'm so ready to get all Donald Trump on a bunch of younger *chicas*. Please, let me be the one who says, 'You're fired!'"

Alicia looked out at Carmen's little sisters playing around in the rowboat. "That's not a bad idea."

Never one to be shy, Jamie said, "Are you kidding? It's a *genius* idea."

Alicia gave her friend a playful shove. "Okay, it's a *genius* idea. So what do we call this brainstorm?"

"Amiga Apprentice?" Carmen said.

Alicia shook her head. "Nah, too derivative."

"Countdown to the *Quince* All-Stars?" Jamie suggested.

Alicia considered it. "That's pretty good."

Carmen smiled. "No, no, I've got it." She drew a few graffiti-style words on a piece of paper and held the sign up so her friends could see:

ARE YOU THAT CHICA?

Alicia smiled. "I love it."

Jamie did, too. And with the name agreed upon, the search for the next leaders of Amigas Inc. began.

The next day, the girls put Are You That Chica? signs up all over the school.

HEY, SOPHOMORES!

Make Money, Have Fun, & Get a Kick-Butt Extracurricular for Your College Applications

ARE YOU THAT CHICA?

Are you the type of girl who always knows the hottest spots and styles?

Are you responsible with money and ready to take those biz skills to the next level?

Do you adore *quinces*, Sweet Sixteens, and festive occasions of all kinds?

Then there might be a place for you with Amigas Inc., Miami's preeminent teen party-planning business.

E-mail 300 words telling us why you're that chica to: AmigasInc@gmail.com

CHAPTER 9

THE NEXT MORNING, Alicia sat on a bench on the quad, reading through the 267 e-mail messages that had flooded the Amigas Inc. in-box. Sure, she looked impeccably well put together in a sky blue fisherman's sweater and a flirty floral miniskirt. But looks can be deceiving. She was seriously and totally stressed out.

Sometimes the reality of how big their *quince* business had gotten just blew her away. Each party took a lot of work, and often Alicia felt as if she needed a degree in family psychology to manage the dynamics of these huge events. For each *quince*, it was her job to assure the parents that the partners in Amigas Inc. really were old enough and responsible enough to plan the most important birthday their young daughter would ever have. After that, there was the drama of the *quince* itself—planning a timeline for the event, choosing a theme and a venue, hiring a staff, making and buying dresses for the girl and her *damas,* and, most challenging of all, gearing up for the inevitable *quince*-zilla meltdown.

It didn't matter if the girl was the calmest, most laid-back *chica* in the universe. Inevitably, there was a moment when she snapped—if only because she was so uncomfortable with all the attention and fuss. The Amigas Inc. team had experienced that exact kind of "please, no more drama" scene with Valeria, a client of theirs from Austin, Texas. Valeria had followed her own indie beat; she was a girl who loved horses and skateboarding with equal passion. Alicia and her friends had had to work overtime to convince Valeria that a *quinceañera* could be a uniquely personal experience that had nothing to do with tiaras or princess dresses.

But even after Valeria had fallen in love with the stylish dress that Carmen had designed for her and the cool ramp Jamie had constructed for her, she had still had a momentary entrance freak-out.

Entrances and exits were always some of the toughest things to coordinate in a *quince*, Alicia believed. Every girl wanted to step out looking beautiful and confident, the best version of herself ever. And at the end of the night, every girl wanted to feel like Cinderella in a contemporary version of the story, where she was not forced to go chase a pumpkin for a ride home. While the girls were whizzes at organization and creativity, the quality that really set them apart from other *quince* planners was their youth; they could identify with their clients, because they knew exactly how it felt to be fifteen.

Alicia thought, *That's why I'm struggling. I can't seem to manage my entrances and exits. Senior year is like being booted from the ball, and applying to college is like not knowing where in the world that pumpkin is going to take you.*

It was still half an hour before homeroom when Jamie approached, looking New York stylish in a cream fedora with a black band; a black T-shirt; skinny jeans; and black platform pumps. "Hey, what's up?" she asked as she handed Alicia a *café con leche.*

"Hey, thanks for the coffee; I need it. I'm so sleepy," Alicia muttered. "Where's Carmen?"

"She and Maxo had to give a tour to middle school students from a mentoring program that Maxo is involved in," Jamie replied.

"Had to or volunteered?" Alicia groaned. She knew that everyone in their group had other obligations. But on days like this, when they had an early-morning

Amigas Inc. meeting, she got a little annoyed if everyone wasn't there.

Jamie shrugged. "Who knows? But I don't think I have the energy to deal with this contest, and let's be honest, who could replace us?"

Patricia Reinoso and her best friend and cousin, Carolina, approached the girls.

"Hey, can we sit with you, or are you doing SAT prep?" Carolina asked.

"Yeah," Patricia chimed in. "You *chicas* look *stressed*."

Alicia explained that they were completely overwhelmed by the prospect of having to search for the next group of girls to run Amigas Inc.

"We're swamped, and we really need to recruit some help—not just to take over the business, but to help plan our mystery *quince*," Jamie explained.

"What's the mystery *quince*?" Carolina asked. "That's a cool theme."

Alicia smiled. "It's not *what*; it's *who*. All we have is a series of anonymous e-mails from the family secretary, Julia Centavo."

Patricia rubbed her hands together excitedly. "Oooh, such intrigue. I love it!"

"Do you have any idea who she is?" Carolina asked.

Jamie exchanged *Can we trust them?* glances with Alicia, and Alicia nodded.

"We actually think it's Carmela Ortega," Jamie said proudly.

"Get out!" Carolina screeched.

Jamie looked around as if there might be *quince* spies everywhere. *"Shhh,"* she whispered. "You can't tell a soul."

"Of course not," Patricia promised.

Carolina blushed at the thought of her earlier outburst. "I'm as silent as the grave."

"So, how can we help?" Patricia asked. "We're juniors, and we are so not swamped."

Carolina looked thrilled at the idea of participating, "Since you planned our *doble quince*, we know what kind of skills it takes to pull this thing off."

Alicia had never even thought about asking the Reinoso cousins for help, even though she liked both of the girls very much. In the months since their double *quince*, Carolina and Patricia had become good friends with the *amigas*—joining them for swims at Alicia's and shopping trips to South Beach. Alicia's father was always saying that a strong leader doesn't try to do every task herself; she delegates to people she trusts and gives them the tools they need to get the job done well. Alicia trusted both Patricia and Carolina. Maybe they *could* be of help.

"Could you guys go through these e-mails and pick—I don't know, the top twenty?" Alicia asked.

"Sure!" Carolina exclaimed.

"We'd love to," added Patricia. She mimicked strutting down an imaginary runway, then struck a fierce and fabulous pose. She spoke as if looking into an imaginary camera. "Are you that *chica*? *We'll* be the judge of that."

Jamie shook her head. "No way; this isn't *America's Next Top Model*. This is serious business. We can't keep girls on the roster just because we want to see the mayhem and the foolishness. We need to cut the *locas* right away. We'll meet the top twelve."

Alicia said, "I'll text you the log-in details for the Amigas Inc. e-mail account right now."

"Cool, got it." Carolina flashed a smile as she checked her phone for the deets. "So, when do you need a list of finalists?"

Alicia opened the calendar on her iPad. "We take the SATs on October twenty-seventh. We could meet on Monday the twenty-ninth. Pick the winners by November fifth. Big day of the *quince* is December fifteenth. And because it's *my* birthday on December sixteenth, I think I'll take a daylong nap."

Jamie was always impressed by the way her friend could juggle a dozen things at once. "Watching you plan a *quince* is like watching a math whiz do some sort of crazy problem in his head," Jamie declared. "It's freaky and impressive at the same time."

The homeroom bell rang, and the girls said their good-byes. As Alicia walked to her classroom, she thought about how lucky she was to have such a capable group of friends. Sure, she might occasionally act as if the business were a one-woman show. But she knew that the real reason Amigas Inc. rocked was that they were all stars. It would be fun, she decided, to have Carolina and Patricia sit in on this mystery *quince* show.

CHAPTER 10

WHILE CAROLINA AND Patricia waded through the masses of wannabe *quince* planners, the owners of Amigas Inc. applied themselves to some heavy-duty SAT prep. The plan was that every day after school, for the two weeks heading up to the exam, they would meet at the school library.

"It has to be at the library," Carmen insisted. "At my house, the racket my little sisters make is too distracting. At Lici's house, the pool is too distracting. We always *say* we're going to study and swim, but we always end up swimming, then not studying."

"What about my place?" Jamie asked.

"I have one word for you." Carmen grinned.

Alicia looked at her friend, "I think I'm thinking of the same can't-study-at-Jamie's-because-it's-too-distracting word."

In unison, Carmen and Alicia cried, "eBay!"

It was the first Thursday in October and the perfect day to launch a massive SAT study attack, because it was a half day of school. Classes ended at one, and the girls knew they could get a good four hours of studying in before their eyes rolled back in their heads and their brains stopped working.

They sat at a large table in the back of the library—away from the watchful glance of Ms. Halisi, the school's head librarian. It was only a few weeks before the SATs, and the room was humming with seniors trying to get ready. It wasn't that the librarian maintained a strict no-talking rule. It was more that Ms. Halisi had a no-laughing-in-the-library rule, which Alicia, Jamie, and Carmen found particularly hard to comply with.

The *amigas* had all done well on the PSATs, the practice-run College Board tests that students took during junior year. And as a result, every day their mailboxes were flooded with packets and brochures from colleges and universities across the country. Yet the *P* in PSAT had made the test seem totally not intimidating. The SATs, on the other hand, were such a critical factor in getting into a good college that Alicia liked to think that the *S* in SATs stood for "sink or swim."

She glanced across the wooden desk at Carmen. Her friend looked as miserable as she felt.

"Why do we have to take a standardized test?" Jamie mused, staring down at her nails, which she had painted bright green with little white golf tees in honor of Dash's upcoming tournament. "There's nothing standard about us!"

Alicia agreed. "I have no idea. I wish the test was all essays. I cannot wait to write my application essays. That's the one part I know I will rock."

"Of course, you would," Carmen whispered to her friend as Ms. Halisi walked by. "You're Miss Verbal Expression. If only I could sketch my entire college application. I could do a darling little capsule collection called Freshman Year at Parsons School of Design."

Alicia loved her friend's creativity. "That would be cool. But even art schools want SAT scores."

"But *why*?" Carmen whined, uncharacteristically for her.

Alicia cracked open the book of SAT practice tests. "I don't know why. But I do know that while we have the *skillz that pay billz*, none of us have photographic memories. So we should start studying. Okay. First question: The policeman exhibited a heedless attitude when dealing with the senior citizen who had just jaywalked across the street. *Heedless* means: A. thoughtless; B. pleasant; C. friendly; D. bitter."

Jamie looked wistfully out the bright picture window and said, "Remind me what we used to do on half-days, back before we were prisoners of the college application system?"

"I will—as soon as you give me the answer," Alicia sighed.

Carmen rested her head on the table and said dreamily, "We used to go to the beach. And we used to go out for frozen yogurt. And we used to go to the mall and take pictures at every photo booth we could find. But that was before, when we were young and carefree."

Ever the diligent student, Alicia saw an opening and took it. "Back when we were *heedless* and young. *Heedless* meaning . . ."

"'Thoughtless,'" Jamie muttered. "As in, it is entirely *heedless* of them to make the practice tests so easy when the actual test is so, so hard."

Alicia couldn't argue with that. "Agreed," she said. "I completely agree."

Carmen looked mischievously at her friends. "I'm not trying to procrastinate. Honest. Well, not much. But I just had the best idea. I have literally, two seconds ago, come up with the best costume idea for Halloween."

During freshman year, the three friends had thrown

around costume ideas for weeks until they finally decided to dress up as members of the Justice League. Carmen was Aquagirl. Jamie was the Green Lantern, and Alicia was Wonder Woman. At fourteen, they'd thought the entire concept was very clever. Then they'd arrived at the first house on their trick-or-treating route to find that there were three Green Lanterns and six Wonder Womans right ahead of them. But the worst was that nobody had ever heard of Aquagirl, so everyone thought Carmen was dressed up like the Little Mermaid, which infuriated her. Gaz, who was at the time just a friend and not yet Alicia's boyfriend, had insisted that their costumes were "genius." But that was Gaz, supportive all the way.

Since that time, the girls had been too busy launching their business to think much about anything social, especially anything that required a costume.

But as Carmen explained, "It's our senior year, and, well, if I do say so myself, it's the end of an era. I know we're busy, but we've got to embrace every fun event that we can all do together."

Alicia closed her SAT book. So much for studying. *Oh, well,* she thought. And as Jamie had said, the practice tests were mad easy. She had gotten a 215 on the PSATs, placing her in the top 2 percent for the state of Florida. But she had felt the need to study, because it was the conscientious thing to do.

"So, Carmen," Alicia wondered aloud, "will you be making our costumes this year?"

"But of course," her friend replied.

Carmen took out her sketchbook and began to draw her idea. Even before she could explain the other-worldly sketches of herself, Alicia, and Jamie, the image of all three of them as ghosts with tiaras had the *amigas* cracking up.

"Twilight in the Garden of Good and *Quince*," Alicia offered, giggling.

Ms. Halisi did not move from her seat, but simply barked a stern "Ladies!"

In deference to this, Carmen whispered, "Not quite *Twilight*. But I thought we could do a little holiday mash-up and steal a page from Charles Dickens. I'll be the ghost of *quinces* past. Alicia, you'll be the ghost of *quinces* present, and Jamie, you're the ghost of *quinces* future."

Jamie smiled. "Does that mean I get to wear an astronaut costume?"

"Absolutely," Carmen beamed.

"Woo-hoo!" Jamie cried, at which point Ms. Halisi took to her feet and came over to their table.

"Given the amount of noise coming from this direction and the fact that your SAT prep book is closed, I am thinking that this would be a good time for you to exit the library," Ms. Halisi declared.

The girls gathered their belongings, a little embarrassed that they'd actually been booted from the premises.

"Do you think we've been banned forever?" Alicia asked earnestly.

"I seriously doubt 'forever,'" Carmen assured her.

"As we are graduating in May, I wouldn't worry about it," Jamie laughed. "Lighten up, Lici!"

The girls were still giggling when Mr. Stevens stopped them in the hall.

"Ladies!" he called out as he approached them.

"That's our name; don't wear it out," Jamie whispered, which only made Carmen and Alicia laugh louder.

"Alicia Cruz. Just the person I was looking for," Mr. Stevens said. His hair flopped down, just a little too long, and his smile was toothpaste-commercial bright. The *amigas* exchanged glances. They didn't actually need to say it. Mr. Stevens was a bit OTT—over the top—but still totally GGC—grown-up-guy cute.

"There's a matter I wanted to discuss with you,"

Mr. Stevens explained. "Could you follow me back to my office?"

Jamie smiled. "Don't tell me! Harvard has already accepted our girl—no application necessary."

Mr. Stevens laughed. "Oh, but if only it were so. Unfortunately, everyone has to do an application for every school, even Ms. Cruz."

Alicia waved to her friends. "Hey, I'll meet you guys at the quad in the morning. Last one in buys the lattes!"

Sitting in Mr. Stevens's office, Alicia felt a wave of apprehension. An exceptionally good student, she'd spent precious little time in the administrative offices. Although she knew she wasn't in any kind of trouble, the fact that Mr. Stevens wanted to see her and had in fact been looking for her made her a little nervous.

She sat up a little straighter as she spoke, channeling Alicia the self-assured *quince* planner. "Hey, Mr. Stevens, what's up?" she asked, putting on the same mature air she tried to project to her clients' parents.

Mr. Stevens pointed to one of the many surfing posters on the wall. "Riding giants, that's what's up."

Alicia was fond of Mr. Stevens, but she had a tough time following everything he said. She had always thought she was familiar with all kinds of slang because she had grown up in multicultural Miami—a city that was known for being an international melting pot. But Mr. Stevens was a math genius/surfer dude, and she hadn't been around his kind enough to catch all of his references.

"Excuse me?" she asked.

Mr. Stevens had on a bright Hawaiian-print golf shirt. Alicia thought he looked as if he'd just gotten off the plane in Maui and was waiting for a local beauty to wrap a lei around his neck. Even though his sense of fashion was corny, he was still definitely cute.

"I know it's short notice," he said. "But I teach this Saturday morning surf class for small-business owners. The new session starts this weekend. It's all about learning how to read the waves—in business and on the beach. It occurs to me that you might like to check it out. There might be some good contacts there for your business. You could learn a few management techniques that would help you with your *quince* planning. . . ."

Alicia was the last person who would have corrected anyone on his or her Spanish pronunciation. But when Mr. Stevens pronounced the word as "kwince," she had to speak up.

"Actually, Mr. S.," she said, "the word *quince* is pronounced 'keen-say.'"

"Whoa. Good to know," he replied, sincerely appreciative. "Thanks. See, you've already taken a page from my soon-to-be-written *Surfboard to Boardroom* business book."

"And what's that?" Alicia asked.

"Be protective of what you value," he replied. "You value your Latina heritage. So you protect it. Just like I value the culture of surfing, so I do my best to protect it. So, will you come on Saturday? I'd love to teach you how to surf."

Alicia was a little apprehensive. Mr. Stevens was cool, but she always pictured surfing as something she'd pick up on some mellow spring-break trip, not during the busiest fall season of her entire life, and not with a group of small-business owners. It sounded as boring as the few chamber of commerce meetings she'd attended. "Um, can I bring two friends?" she asked. "I don't run Amigas Inc. solo."

"Of course!" he replied. "Just make sure your friends are ready to get down, B to B."

Alicia was confused again. "Excuse me?"

"Board to business," Mr. Stevens cheerily explained. "The business of being literally and figuratively on board."

Alicia smiled and looked at her watch. She was due

to meet Gaz at the mall during his break, in half an hour. If she didn't leave soon, she'd be late. But before she could remember the universal symbol for "hang loose, see you later," Mr. Stevens gave her an out.

He stood up and put his hand out for a high five. "Up top, Cruz," he said.

Alicia tried not to look relieved. Surfing lessons in the middle of her megabusy senior year? She'd have to find a polite way to get out of them. She gave Mr. Stevens a high five and went off to meet her boyfriend.

CHAPTER 11

THE CRUZ FAMILY room was a big open space that consisted of a kitchen and a living-and-dining space. The room had floor-to-ceiling windows on one side and a glass door that led out to the pool. Alicia's parents collected photographs by Latin American artists; the walls were covered with brightly colored depictions of men, women, and children from places ranging from Mexico City to Montevideo. The family's schedule was increasingly hectic, but with Alicia's older brother off at college, her mother insisted that they eat dinner together at least three days a week. This was one of those nights.

Although Alicia complained about her mother's summoning her home when she really wanted to grab a bite with Gaz or her friends, she loved the family dinners. And ever since Maribelle had started dating Hiro, a chef at Nobu Miami Beach, the family had been treated to an array of new and impressive Japanese meals. Tonight, the menu consisted of *nabe udon*, a big clay hot pot of noodles and seafood.

Alicia's parents often changed before dinner, but it had been a busy week. Her father had barely had time to loosen his tie before sitting down, and her mother had come dashing in from a meeting that had run late; she had quickly kicked off her pumps and made a giant bib out of a linen napkin, so as not to spill anything on her silk blouse.

Alicia felt like the parent as she sat patiently at the table waiting for them. "Relax," she said, using on them the word they had used on her for years. "The food's not going to run off the table." Her mother and father laughed.

"Where have I heard that advice before?" Mrs. Cruz teased.

As Alicia filled her bowl, she told her parents about her college adviser. "He's like a surf dude in a suit who's really good at math."

"That doesn't sound so bad to me," her mother replied.

Her father agreed. "Sounds like a well-balanced guy."

Alicia sighed. "Well, he wants me to come to a surf class he's teaching on Saturday."

"Is it for C. G. High students?" her mother asked.

"Nope, it's for small-business owners," Alicia explained. "It's some 'ride the wave, be on board,' business/surfing thing he does. I really don't want to go. I just haven't figured out a way out of it."

"What a wonderful opportunity," her mother said, in between bites of udon noodles.

"And a real honor to be asked," her father added.

Alicia poured herself a glass of cold green tea. "I know, I know. But for some reason, I'm a little nervous," she admitted. "Hopefully I can convince Carmen and Jamie to go with me."

Somehow, her mother had managed to make the big napkin tucked into her blouse look elegant—stylish, even. "You know it's good to get out of your comfort zone sometimes," she asserted. Then, segue-ing a little awkwardly to a more pressing matter, she added, "Speaking of which, how are those college applications going?"

Alicia shrugged and tapped her chopsticks against her plate. "It's all fine," she mumbled.

Her mother looked concerned. It wasn't like Alicia to be so evasive. Even so, and despite their own high-achieving careers, Marisol and Enrique Cruz made every effort not to be pushy when it came to their kids.

This was a delicate balance—nurturing success without demanding it.

The awkward silence that filled the room was indicative of what everyone felt.

Marisol broke the ice. "So, Lici, is the list of schools you're applying to the same as it was last time we talked?" she asked her daughter gently.

"Um, yeah," Alicia muttered, helping herself to a couple of Maribelle's homemade shrimp dumplings.

Her parents exchanged glances. Mrs. Cruz had tried. Now it was Mr. Cruz's turn.

Enrique took a deep breath, then plunged ahead. "We're old and slightly senile," he joked. This was, of course, patently untrue. He was not yet fifty. "Let's go over the list together," he suggested, "just for the benefit of the memory-challenged among us. It's Brown, Columbia, Penn, Yale, and that dinky little school up in Cambridge. . . ."

In spite of herself, Alicia smiled at her dad's corny sense of humor.

"Harvard," she said, finishing his sentence.

"Oh, right, Harvard," her father beamed. "Didn't the rep invite you to coffee?"

"Yeah, I've got to call her," Alicia replied nonchalantly. She'd kept Serena Shih's business card on her dresser, and she looked at it every day. As soon as she figured out what to say besides *I really, really want to go to Harvard*, she planned to give her a ring.

Sensing that Alicia was not enthused about the college conversation, her mother changed the topic. "So, how are things going with the mystery *quince*?"

Alicia smiled. In spite of all the stress and pressure of senior year, the idea of planning a *quince* for Carmela Ortega was *very* exciting. "We haven't heard from Julia Centavo in a while, which is good, because we're hoping to hire some sophomores to help us out and to take over the day-to-day operations when we go away to college."

"Right," her mother said. "I ran into Jamie's mom, and she told me you were having a contest to find your successors, called Are You That *Chica*?"

Her father reached for his briefcase and handed Alicia a section of the newspaper. "I saved this for you. Yesenia and Carmela Ortega are out of the country—on a diplomatic trip to South Korea."

Alicia's eyes widened as she looked at the picture in the paper of Carmela Ortega and her mother wearing traditional Korean dresses. "How cool is this?" she asked her parents excitedly. "I cannot *wait* to meet them."

Her mother held one hand up, in a gesture of

caution. "Don't get your hopes up, Lici," she warned. "You don't know for sure that she's your mystery client."

But Alicia wouldn't be swayed. "She is. Deep down in my gut it feels right. After all, our birthdays are just one day apart. We share the same astrological sign, which means we're both awesome. I already feel like I know her."

"So, have you decided on a theme yet?" her mother asked.

"Not yet," Alicia said. "But we've got a little time. Usually, when we have enough time to plan, the budget is small and we spend all our time wheeling and dealing. If the budget is big, the client always wants it all done yesterday, so we're rushing around like madwomen. This *quince* is a happy medium—generous budget, reasonable timeline."

Alicia's parents looked at each other and laughed.

"What is it?" Alicia wanted to know.

"It's just that, four years ago, you had braces and your biggest ambition was to show off your dancing skills on a reality TV show," her mother said teasingly.

Alicia playfully lobbed a napkin at her mom and replied, "Oh, nice. Well, for your information, four years ago, I was thirteen, and I was, and still am, an excellent dancer! I could so be on TV."

Her father smiled and squeezed his daughter's shoulder. He said, "What your mother is trying to say is that we are really proud of you. You've not only built a thriving business; you've helped us all see an old tradition with new eyes. That's really special. That takes vision."

Alicia stood up and hugged each of her parents. She didn't say anything, because it was one of those moments when she knew that they understood exactly how she felt. As the saying went, *sin palabras*. There were simply no words.

CHAPTER 12

THE FOLLOWING Saturday morning, Alicia stood on the beach, shivering in her wet suit. When Mr. Stevens had mentioned his surfing class, he hadn't said anything about being encased in rubber and on the beach at six a.m. As she looked around at the group of men and women twice her age, she wondered how she'd let her girls off the hook so easily. Jamie was traveling to see Dash compete in a tournament in Orlando, and Carmen had flat-out not wanted to go.

"I like surf-inspired fashion," Carmen had said. "Like the cool T's and cute dresses designers like Cynthia Rowley have been doing. I like listening to surf-inspired ska, and I *love* old nineteen-fifties surfing movies. What I don't like—and can't see happening—is me, trying to stand on a board in freezing cold water while said board knocks me upside the head every time I fall off it."

Wow, Alicia remembered thinking. *Way to sell it, Carmen.* Now she wondered if her friend hadn't been *absolutamente y completamente* right. It was chilly, it was still a little dark, and the ocean did not look either fun or inviting.

Mr. Stevens, however, didn't seem to mind the cold or the hour. "Good morning!" he bellowed as he jogged happily toward the sullen-looking group, some of whom were hopping from one foot to the other in an attempt to stay warm. "Welcome to Surfing the New Economy! You are a very special group of people, and not just because you're all dressed in these neoprene penguin suits! You are all business owners. Why don't you each go ahead and introduce yourselves?"

There were eight people in the group; Alicia was the youngest by far.

A tall guy with red hair, who looked about her father's age, stepped forward confidently and said, "Hi, I'm Dave, of Dave's Honey Wagons. We rent trailers to celebrities who are shooting in Miami—movies, TV commercials, music videos—you name it."

Alicia was impressed and immediately began thinking about how she could incorporate trailers used by real movie stars into a *quinceañera* theme.

Next, a woman with dark brown shoulder-length

hair and deep dimples smiled at the group and said, "I'm, Maya, the owner of Buscar, a new age bookshop and café in West Park." She clasped her hands together and did a little bow. *"Namaste,"* she told the group.

The rest had equally interesting pursuits—from a cupcake shop to a pharmacy that had been the family business for over a hundred years.

When it was Alicia's turn, she found that she wasn't as cold as she had been when she had first arrived. The sun was shining more brightly, and she no longer felt so shy.

"*Hola*, everybody," she said, waving at the small group. "I'm Alicia, and I'm the cofounder of Amigas Inc., a full-service *quinceañera* planning business."

Everyone seemed surprised that someone as young as Alicia could have her own business.

"Excuse me," a woman named Terri, who owned a Pilates studio, said, "but would it be rude for me to ask your age?"

Alicia smiled. "Not at all. I'm seventeen."

"And how long have you had this business?" Dave wondered.

"For two years," Alicia replied.

"Impressive!" Dave said brightly.

"Have you ever thought of taking your *quince*

business national?" asked Lily, who owned the cupcake shop. "My sister lives in San Antonio, and I know they could use something like this out there."

All of a sudden, Alicia felt the pride that had been eluding her since the beginning of senior year. Maybe she didn't have the musical talent that Gaz had; she certainly didn't have Jamie's artistic gifts; and she couldn't sketch or sew like Carmen (then again, who could?). But what she'd done with the help of her oh-so-talented friends was to start a business that could actually go national, a business that could potentially last a very long time.

The group chatted for a few minutes, and then Mr. Stevens interrupted. "Okay, people, now it's time to do the work," he announced. "Your first exercise is a pop-up." As if it were the easiest thing in the world, he jumped onto the sand, landed in a full push-up, and from there, jumped back to a standing position. "*That* is essentially how you stand up on a surfboard.

"Now, everybody try it," he suggested cheerfully.

They did, and, from the sloppy scrambles to the ground, coupled with a few real moans and groans, Alicia could tell that everyone found the exercise quite as difficult as she did.

The beach was getting more crowded, and soon the

would-be surfers were sharing their turf with couples out together for an early-morning stroll and others walking their dogs. Alicia tried to fight her self-consciousness.

Mr. Stevens asked the group, "So, where did you feel that exercise?"

People called out answers ranging from "my legs" to "my hips" to, oddly enough, "my ankles."

Mr. Stevens pointed to his stomach. "Where you should be feeling it is right here. Surfing is all about using your core. And this is where what you learn on the board will help you become chairman or chairwoman of the board. Because in business, as in life, you've got to trust your gut." Then he said, "Okay, folks, give me fifteen pop-ups."

Alicia did ten pop-ups and thought her arms would drop off, or her legs, or both.

Next thing she knew, she was in the ocean, sitting on top of her board and gazing out at the horizon. The sound of the bright blue waves echoed the churning that she felt inside. There was so much to think about: the future of Amigas Inc.; her relationship with Gaz; college . . . As she paddled out further, she considered Mr. Stevens's recommendation: *Trust your gut.* Alicia felt that his message had been for her and only her. Was her gut telling her something that she had been trying hard to ignore? She took a deep breath and closed her eyes.

Suddenly, she knew. Harvard was her first-choice school. That was where she wanted to be. Not because it was where her parents had gone or because it was where everyone expected her to go, but because it was the best place for a young entrepreneur like herself. She was so happy she wanted to hug Mr. Stevens.

The group had barely gotten the hang of paddling out when the two-hour class was over.

Afterward, Mr. Stevens, all grins, asked her, "So, what do you think? You didn't want to come, did you? I really wasn't sure you would show up."

Alicia looked shyly down at her bare feet. "I think I loved it. And you were right about learning to read the waves. Out on the water, I suddenly felt so strong and calm. I've been struggling for so long to decide which college felt like the best fit for me, and now I know for certain that Harvard is my first choice."

Mr. Stevens crossed his arms in front of his chest. "Well, that's interesting news. You know, I get my best ideas when I'm out in the ocean."

Alicia nodded. She wasn't ready to ride a giant just yet; she was more a baby-stepping surfing wannabe. But she'd gone beyond her comfort zone, and that small move had made everything else seem possible.

"I know it *here*," she said, pointing to her stomach. "In my gut. I also don't want to apply just to Ivy League schools. I want to target schools that will help me nurture my creativity and business skills. Schools that have innovative programs where I can meet cool people like I met today."

Mr. Stevens patted her on the shoulder. "Alicia, girl, I think you just caught your first big wave."

Later that morning, Alicia arrived at home to find her parents swimming in the pool. It always surprised her to see them just chilling like a couple of teenagers. Her parents usually just sat by the pool. Her father liked to read international newspapers on his Kindle, and her mother was surgically attached to her BlackBerry. But for Marisol and Enrique Cruz to be *in* their swimsuits, *in* the water? Not so much.

Alicia kicked off her flip-flops and sat at the edge of the pool, letting her legs dangle in the water.

"*¡Hola, gente!*" she announced, beckoning to her parents the way her father had used to call out to her and her brother when he wanted to get their attention.

They swam over, amused expressions on their faces.

"I have an announcement," Alicia proclaimed. "Harvard has a joint BA/MBA program that I'm really excited about. It's going to be my first-choice school."

Her mother was smiling so broadly that Alicia couldn't help teasing her. "Mom, relax! You look like one of those Botoxed South Beach ladies."

Marisol Cruz splashed her, despite the fact that Alicia was fully dressed, in a very cute boatneck T and denim shorts.

"Can't a mother be proud?" her mom asked.

Alicia blushed. "Mom, for real, chill. Let me get into Harvard first."

Her father might not have been a practicing lawyer anymore, but he still knew how to cross-examine a witness. "Lici," he ventured, "you've been so secretive about college applications. Is there something we should know?"

Alicia sighed. She remembered how brave she had felt paddling out on her rented longboard into the big blue ocean, and she knew she was brave enough, finally, to tell her parents the truth.

"Hey, I don't want to turn this into some big, deep moment," she began, "but the truth is I've been really conflicted about applying to Harvard. You guys are so successful; it's a lot to live up to. I've been fighting Harvard, because I didn't want to just follow in your footsteps. I wanted to achieve something on my own."

Her parents looked shocked, as if they had just spotted her on TV in some "Secret Life of Teenagers" documentary special.

"Lici!" her father exclaimed. "You are seventeen years old and you've started a business that grosses more than I made my first year out of college."

Her mother put on a robe and sat down next to her at the edge of the pool. Reflexively, Alicia rested her head on her mother's shoulder.

"You are a complete original," her mother said. "There's no limit to what you can do. Your father and I have been fortunate. We've done well, and we're grateful for that. But our dream was never just to give you and your brother a fancy house with a swimming pool. Our goal—our desire—was to have enough to give you choices, to show you all the possibilities the world has to offer. But with your *quince* business, you have shown *us* what our own culture and heritage have to offer."

In spite of herself, Alicia started crying. Her mother joined her. Out of the corner of her eye, Alicia could see that her father was tearing up, too. "Are you crying, Papa?" she asked.

Enrique dived underneath the water and spiraled back up to the surface. "I'm not crying," he sniffed.

Then, in a more serious tone, he said to his daughter, "You are my best gift."

Alicia, ever the little sister, asked, "What about Alex?"

Her father guffawed. "When he comes home from college and mows the lawn, he can be my best gift, too."

That night, before she went to sleep, Alicia texted all of her friends.

The message read: *Big announcement. Figured out my college dream. Applying to Harvard, their joint ba/mba program rocks. Next step: amigas inc. omnimedia.*

She hit SEND with an excited flourish. It felt so good just to be putting the idea out there.

Carmen wrote: *Love it, amiga!*

Gaz wrote: *Boston or bust, mi amor!*

Maxo wrote: *We'll all be working for you one day. (the title I want is: chief technical officer.)*

And of course, Jamie had to put her sassy spin on the whole thing: *You and Harvard are like peanut butter and jelly. No-brainer, Lici.*

It was fabulous, Alicia thought as she crawled into bed. Now, all she had to do was get accepted.

CHAPTER 13

A FEW WEEKS LATER, Alicia's college drama had calmed down considerably. Alicia and her friends had gotten through the SATs, and while they'd all found them harder than the practice tests, they were all fairly confident that they'd done well. With the help of Mr. Stevens, Alicia had not only stood up for a whole ten seconds on her longboard, she'd also added UC Berkeley, NYU, and the University of Michigan to the list of colleges she was applying to. With their applications well under way, the girls were finally about to turn their attention back to the mystery *quince*. This was good, because during the last week of October, they received an e-mail from Julia Centavo:

Dear Amigas Inc.,

We are looking forward to receiving the detailed proposal for my client's *quince* on November 1st, as promised. We trust that you've had a good semester. The young woman I work for has been very busy, but now her schedule has cleared and we hope to get biweekly check-ins from your team for her review.

Cordialmente,
Julia Centavo

It was October 30, and the three partners in Amigas Inc. were embarrassed to admit that in the rush of schoolwork, college applications, and, in Alicia's case, surfing lessons, they had, uncharacteristically, neglected to do almost any work on Carmela Ortega's *quince*. It was time to move into high gear. With this in mind, Alicia texted Carolina and Patricia Reinoso: *Chicas, hope you've found some good potentials for us because we need help and fast!*

Carolina Reinoso wrote back right away: *Can you meet us at the quad after school? 3 pm?*

Alicia answered: *Claro, see you then.*

At three p.m. sharp, Alicia, Jamie, and Carmen arrived at their favorite bench in the quad, to find that Carolina and Patricia were already there. The normally casual and relaxed Reinoso girls were both formally dressed in pin-striped pants and button-down shirts. They both looked nervous.

Jamie, never one to beat around the bush, prodded them. "Is there a problem? Because my Spidey sense is telling me something is up."

Patricia took a deep breath and said, "We read each and every application—all two hundred sixty-seven of them. And we want to be perfectly honest: there were a few decent candidates. . . ."

Carolina jumped in. "But we don't think you should hire any of them. You should hire *us*."

Alicia, Carmen, and Jamie were more than surprised. While they had all enjoyed the friendship that had developed with the Reinoso cousins over the past few months, they still put them in the category of fabulous former clients, like Dash's sister, Binky Mortimer.

Jamie was immediately and categorically against the idea. "But you guys are our friends. What we're looking for is minions—worker bees! Sophomores who will be at our beck and call! Girls whom we could easily cut loose if they don't work out. Hiring you two is definitely not what I had in mind." Pouting, she took a seat on the opposite bench. Then, as was her wont, she took out her iPhone and began texting Dash.

Alicia turned to Carmen and asked, "What do you think?"

Carmen thought for a moment and then turned to the younger girls. "Well, I love you both, and not just because you campaigned to have me elected queen of the winter formal last year! But part of the reason we were aiming for sophomores was that we wanted to pick people who could run the business for two years. When you graduate next year, we'll be right back where we started."

Carolina sighed. "We know. And that's a totally valid point."

Patricia turned to Jamie. "And I feel you, *chica*. I kind of would love to have some sophomore underlings myself."

Carolina continued, "But as we read the applications, we couldn't help but think that Amigas Inc. isn't just some school club that is run out of the activities office with an interchangeable string of elected leaders. This is a serious business, and it's a serious opportunity. Honestly, I don't think you want minions. I think you want business partners, people who can represent both you and the cultural institution of *quinceañeras*. We would do that."

Carmen tugged at Alicia's sleeve. "So what do you

think, Alicia? You're the head *chica* in charge."

Alicia paused. It was flattering, really, that girls as cool as Carolina and Patricia wanted to be part of the business. But she had questions, lots of them. "Patricia, you're the star of the school basketball team, and Carolina, you're a cheerleader and head of the environmental club. How will you juggle Amigas Inc. with the rest of your extracurricular activities *and* school?"

Carolina said, "Part of what's so attractive to us about this opportunity is that it's a chance for us to distinguish ourselves next fall, when we're in your position, applying for colleges. Patricia's got more going on than I do. She's a talented athlete. But at the end of the day, there are hundreds of high school basketball players, cheerleaders, and school club presidents applying to college every year. How many of those students can say that they are also successful entrepreneurs?"

Alicia nodded. She loved to hear other people talk about how great the Amigas Inc. business was. She felt that, if she said it, she'd have been bragging about herself and her friends. But when someone like Carolina, or Serena Shih from Harvard, said it, that was totally different—it was indicative of how meaningful the work really was.

Patricia chimed in, "We've been looking for a

project we can work on together. To tell you the truth, when we were growing up, we spent nearly every waking hour running in and out of each other's houses. Then we came to high school, and it's like we live in different worlds. But the fact is, we love our Latina heritage, we want to learn more about different cultural traditions, and working on Amigas Inc. seems like a great way to bring all of that together."

Alicia started to speak. "Well—"

But Patricia interrupted her. "Wait, there's more! We'd like to offer to take the lead on the mystery *quince*, under your supervision. And if you find us lacking, then no harm, no foul. You'll have the whole spring semester to find some different successors."

Carolina reached into her very stylish tote bag and took out three folders. She gave one to each of the *amigas*.

"What's this?" Alicia asked.

Carolina explained. "It's a proposal for Carmela Ortega's *quinceañera*, with suggested themes, venues, colors, favors, catering, stationery options . . ."

Alicia flipped through the proposal. It seemed very thorough, but she was beginning to think it was awkward to discuss the pros and cons of handing the business over to Carolina and Patricia right in front of them.

She looked up at the cousins and said, "This is amazing; thank you. But I think the executive committee needs to meet—"

Jamie stopped texting and asked, "Wait a second, who's the executive committee?"

Carmen resisted the urge to roll her eyes. "She means us! You, me, and Lici."

Jamie returned to her phone mumbling, "Oh, yeah, right."

Alicia smiled at Carolina and Patricia. "Excuse my friend. Her boyfriend's away at college, and it's like she just discovered social networking. Give us a chance to meet and discuss these ideas. Carmela Ortega is a very important client, and we have to weigh all of this carefully."

Carolina stood up and extended her hand for Alicia to shake. "Thank you for your consideration."

Alicia resisted the urge to laugh. Even more than Patricia, it was clear that Carolina was taking the whole enterprise superseriously. Although Carolina was an A student and spearheaded the environmental club, the students of C.G. clearly saw her as the popular blond cheerleader, an identity that was not completely to her liking. Alicia understood that Carolina viewed working for Amigas Inc. as an opportunity to prove that she was more than just a pretty, perky girl. Alicia could respect that. After all, hadn't part of what drove her to create the business been the desire to show that she was more than the sheltered daughter of two supersuccessful Miami professionals?

The *amigas* had barely walked away when Carolina came running after them. "One more thing," she said, slightly out of breath. She reached into her bag and grabbed three more folders. "I know you guys need options. Here's a list of our top twelve choices among the applicants, with our assessments of their strengths, weaknesses, and what they could offer Amigas Inc."

Now Alicia was really impressed. A studied analysis of the competition was not something most girls would offer up. It was one thing to put together a proposal for a *quince*. Every girl she'd known, especially those who'd had big *quinceañera* celebrations, relished the idea of giving advice about someone else's big day. In a way, it was a chance to relive the celebration, making new and different choices. Sometimes, Alicia thought the reason she got so crazily possessive about the business was that she was the only one in the group who'd never had a *quinceañera*.

Way back when she was fourteen, she'd made the decision to take a trip to Spain with Carmen and her family to celebrate her fifteenth birthday, rather than have a big, expensive party. At the time, she had attended literally dozens of corny *quinces* with girls who wore too much makeup and took the whole occasion as an excuse to get dolled up in big poufy dresses with more layers than a wedding cake. She hadn't known back then how cool a *quince* could be. Ever since, as she had helped her friends and clients plan theirs, she was always a little sorry that, back when it had been time for her special day, she hadn't thought to break with tradition, to do the kind of modern and meaningful ceremony for which Amigas Inc. was now so well known.

How did that expression go? Alicia all at once remembered—*Necessity is the mother of invention.* She'd invented the kind of cool, big-sister party-planning business that would have made all the difference when she herself was considering having a *quinceañera.* But it was too late now. What mattered was making sure that Carmela Ortega had a *quince* that was both memorable and meaningful, and that the partners in Amigas Inc. entrusted their business to someone—or some group of someones—who would do the business proud.

CHAPTER 14

THAT SATURDAY, Alicia woke up at seven to find the house unusually silent. Then she remembered. Maribelle had the day off, and her parents had attended a big political fund-raiser the night before. They would undoubtedly be sleeping in. It was rare to have the house almost to herself. So she changed into her swimsuit, went out, and tiptoed toward the pool.

She rarely ever did laps anymore, but in the quiet of the morning, it felt good just to swim silently from one end of the pool to the other. Mr. Stevens was at a weekend economics conference, so there was no Surfing the New Economy class. And while the Cruz family pool was no substitute for the Atlantic Ocean, as she did her laps, she could close her eyes and picture herself paddling out and imagine the feel and taste of the salt water on her lips and skin.

When she was done swimming, it was eight a.m.,

and she figured it was now not too early to text Jamie and Carmen. *Hey, you guys, want to come over for breakfast and discuss the proposal? I'm making waffles.*

Alicia did not do much cooking, mostly because anything she might have made would have paled in comparison with the culinary masterpieces that Maribelle turned out on the regular. Still, ever since she was a kid, Alicia had loved making waffles. She must have been seven when Maribelle had first taught her how to make the batter and, holding her hand, let her pour it into the electric waffle iron. As she got older, she had experimented more and more with the ingredients. Sometimes she did just fruit, cutting up blueberries, strawberries, and bing cherries when she had them. Then she went through a sweet phase, adding chocolate chips, caramel swirls, even bits of marshmallow. Finally, she combined it all to make what she called an everything waffle, which was everything that she loved, all mixed into one big lump of battery goodness: strawberries, chocolate chips, marshmallows, and bits of almond and toffee for a bit of crunch. It was delicious. And while Maribelle frowned on this—"You should call it the dentist special! *¡Ay, niña!*"—her friends loved it.

Which was why, despite the earliness of the hour, Alicia soon received two responses for her invitation.

Jamie wrote: *Everything waffles? Give me 20 minutes.*

Carmen wrote: *Yum. On my way.*

Alicia smiled. It was always so much fun to feed her friends. Throwing a robe on over her swimsuit, she went into the kitchen and began to mix up the ingredients.

By the time Carmen and Jamie arrived, Alicia's parents were up; they joined the girls at the breakfast table, in the middle of which was a big stack of everything waffles. And Maribelle had left a tropical fruit salad in the fridge with a note that said, *To counteract the sugary disaster you will concoct in my absence.* Jamie made the coffee—strong, just the way the Cruzes liked it. And Carmen brought over a loaf of her mother's homemade banana bread.

There were a few moments of silence as they all filled their plates and took their first satisfying bites. Then Alicia's mother asked, "So, how goes it with the mystery *quince*?"

Alicia took out the folder that the Reinoso cousins had prepared. "Well, that's actually why I invited Carmen and Jamie over to breakfast. We've got a lot to discuss."

She filled her parents in on Carolina's and Patricia's business proposal, in which the cousins suggested that they apprentice under the three girls for the rest of the school year, then take over when the original members all left for college.

"Well, what do you think of their ideas for the mystery *quince*?" her mother asked, taking a sip of her coffee.

Alicia flipped the folder open. "Well, for one, I love the venue."

The Reinoso girls had suggested that Amigas Inc. rent Chez Gusteau, a fancy French restaurant with stunning views of the airport runways.

"I can't believe we've never thought of having a *quince* there before," Alicia said. "It's so modern, so global chic to be turning fifteen and watching planes take off for destinations all over the world."

Carmen agreed. "It's a wonderful space, and I wonder, do you think the president will loan Carmela Ortega Air Force One?"

Alicia's father almost choked on his waffle. "Do you guys honestly think that the president loans out his *personal*, paid-for-by-taxpayers plane for a teenage girl to travel to her birthday party in Miami?"

Holding the pan with a pot holder, Alicia brought a warm stack of waffles to the table. "It's not just any birthday party," she said. "It's Carmela Ortega's *quince*."

Her father shook his head in mock distress. "*Hijas*, please, take your heads out of the clouds and return to planet earth."

Alicia's mother weighed in. "It doesn't matter. If it is actually her, she and probably many of her guests will be arriving by airplane, so being near the airport will be nice."

"I like the venue," Jamie commented. "Now, does that eliminate the need for us to find a caterer?"

Alicia pulled out a paper-clipped stack of menus. "The Reinoso girls got the chef at the restaurant to propose several different menus. These all look really good to me. We can e-mail them to Julia Centavo. We need the girls to send us an electronic version."

Jamie lifted her phone and said, "Just checked the Amigas Inc. e-mail address. They've already sent an electronic version. So, which menu do you like, Lici? I kind of love the French brasserie menu: the mussels and fries; the mini hamburgers; the mini ham sandwiches."

Alicia considered. It all sounded delicious, but even so, she said, "I like the French Polynesian menu. It's imaginative but sounds really tasty, but formal enough for a sit-down: coconut crabmeat soup, roasted pork and ginger fried rice, pineapple upside-down cake. Yum, pineapple upside-down cake is my *favorite*."

Carmen held up a brightly colored sheet of paper. "Look at this supercute menu of nonalcoholic 'mock-tails.' I love the Tiki hut theme and illustrations."

Alicia examined the drinks menu. "These illustrations read a little young to me. But the idea of a mocktail menu I love, love, love."

Her mother said, "It sounds like you guys are suitably impressed. Are Carolina and Patricia hired?"

Alicia turned to her friends. "*¿Qué piensan?* I think they've gone above and beyond. It's not all ready to go, but it definitely shows they've got a knack for this."

Jamie raised her hand.

"Yes, Jamie?" Alicia asked, amused.

"I'm voting yes, because I've actually got to—" Jamie began.

"Dash," Alicia said, finishing her sentence for her.

"Exactly," Jamie beamed. She gulped down the rest of her orange juice and hugged Alicia's parents.

"Even if we hire the Reinosos, we've actually still got a lot of work to do on Carmela's *quince*," Alicia yelled to Jamie, who was click-clacking down the hall in her kitten heels.

"I know," Jamie called out over her shoulder. "Sign me up for photography, videography, favors, and overall fabulous touches."

Alicia shook her head. If anyone else had made that statement she would've accused them of passing the buck. But she knew that what Jamie promised was exactly what Jamie could be counted on to deliver— especially the "overall fabulous touches."

"So, it's just you and me, Carmen," Alicia observed.

Carmen stood up sheepishly and mumbled, "Can I get a couple of everything waffles to go? Maxo's grandmother is visiting from New York, and I'm trying to make her a blanket of traditional Haitian prayer flags, and let's just say I've bitten off more than I can sew."

Alicia sighed. "But what am I going to do? Julia Centavo is expecting a proposal by Monday."

Carmen squeezed her friend's shoulder, "Well, why don't you make any changes you want to the electronic file and then we'll tell Carolina and Patricia tonight that they are hired and they can do the rest. They are going to be so-o-o-o excited."

"Well, okay," Alicia said.

A few minutes after Carmen left, Alicia heard the doorbell ring. She assumed that Carmen had forgotten something—a scarf or some other accessory she'd made that Alicia would have been perfectly happy to keep. She was surprised to see Gaz at the front door.

He kissed her deeply. "*Hola*, stranger."

She smiled, feeling thankful that she'd brushed her teeth right after breakfast!

"What are you doing here?" she asked.

He grinned. "I was sort of, kind of, not anywhere near here. But I missed you, and I don't have to be at work until four. So I thought I'd drop by."

Alicia pouted. "You don't have to be at work until later, but I've really got to work now. I've got to focus on this proposal for Carmela Ortega's *quince*. Do you have any interest in helping me?" she asked, hopefully.

"That depends," Gaz said flirtatiously. "Do you have any interest in feeding me? Because I will work for food."

Three hours, six everything waffles, two Gorgonzola-stuffed burgers, four cans of Coca-Cola, and half a cheesecake later, this was what Alicia e-mailed her mystery client:

Dear Ms. Centavo,

It is with great pleasure that we offer the following proposal for your client's fifteenth-birthday celebration. As soon as you let us know your preferences, we will begin to finalize the details.

Location:

Chez Gusteau

This traditional French restaurant offers stunning views of planes landing and arriving at Miami International Airport. Double-paned windows ensure that noise is not an issue.

Theme:

Paris Nights, Miami Mornings

Our basic concept is that your client, whoever she is, is a girl of the world. With the Miami airport as our backdrop and the French restaurant as the venue, we think that this theme will give us a lot of room to be creative and will be singularly evocative for both the girl of honor and her guests.

Color scheme:

We envision this as a clean, ultrasophisticated event. We would suggest a sharp black-and-white color scheme, with hot pink as the accent color.

Menu:

The space would be divided into two rooms. The formal dining room, with the theme "Paris Nights," would offer a French-inspired sit-down meal. We are including several menus, including a contemporary French Polynesian fusion menu and a classic Parisian brasserie menu.

The second room would serve as the reception area and then later as the dance space, where, designwise, we would focus on "Miami Mornings." We would also offer a selection of nonalcoholic cocktails, aka "mocktails," with illustrations that would be slightly more sophisticated than what you see here.

Flowers:
Please see the attached JPEGs for samples of bouquets from a new florist we are considering, Garden and Bloom.

Activities and favors:
In the courtyard of the restaurant, in between the reception and the sit-down meal areas, we would like to suggest constructing a backdrop where guests can have their pictures taken. Some thoughts for the backdrop would be a Parisian street scene, a luxury jet, and an image of Miami Beach. Your *quince* and her friends are people who are going places, and they would enjoy posing for these photos, as well as taking small framed photos home as keepsakes at the end of the evening.

After dinner, while a band plays indoors, we would cover the photo backdrop with a white sheet and project a movie in the breezeway of the restaurant. Guests could choose between dancing indoors and gathering on couches to watch a classic Hollywood film. The film would, of course, be of your client's choosing.

Immediate pending items:
1) Dress designs. Will your client be needing a dress? Or will she be bringing one? We have an excellent designer/seamstress on our team.
2) Father-daughter *vals*. How might we help your client with the choreography of this very important element, considering that we are not meeting her until the day of the event?
3) *Damas* and *chambelanes*. Traditionally, the *quince* is attended by a court of seven girls (*damas*) and seven boys (*chambelanes*). How would you like us to handle this group? We usually dress or source their outfits as well as handling any special choreography they might require.
4) Church ceremony. If your client is Catholic: We've worked with some of the most beautiful churches in the area and can arrange meetings as you need them.

Just as Alicia was about to hit SEND, Gaz, who had single-handedly polished off three pieces of cheesecake, shyly said, "I know this client is a big deal. Maybe the biggest deal you've ever represented. But would you feel comfortable presenting my music to her to consider for the performance?"

Alicia paused.

Gaz took her silence for a rejection. He looked down and said, "Hey, Lici, forget I even asked. It's no big deal. You've hooked me and the band up with so many gigs. I understand you've got a very particular concept for this *quince*."

Alicia shook her head. "Oh, no, Gaz. Not at all. I was just thinking about how to present your music as the main option without saying, 'He's my boyfriend and he's awesome.'"

She tapped a few lines out on her laptop.

Music:
We are really proud to have worked a number of times with local singer-songwriter Gaspar Colón. We are confident that he and his band can offer a wide range of musical options, from traditional salsa to more modern compositions and pop covers. Please listen to the enclosed MP3 files and let us know your thoughts.

She read the passage to Gaz and asked, "Does that sound good?"

He hugged her and kissed her again and again. "Better than good, Lici," he replied. "It sounds amazing. This is why I love you. When I'm around you, I feel like I can do anything."

She kissed him playfully on the neck. "Right back atcha, handsome. Not every guy would spend a Saturday afternoon helping his girlfriend put together a proposal for a VIQ."

"Very Important *Quince*?" Gaz guessed.

"Exactly," Alicia smiled, as she sent the e-mail off to Julia Centavo.

"Well, not every guy has a girlfriend who can cook waffles like you and who's so inspiring with all of her ideas," Gaz said.

"So, what you're saying is that we're perfect for each other," Alicia said, winking at him.

"That is exactly what I'm saying," Gaz replied. He stood up, walked over to where she was sitting, and lifted her fingers off the keyboard. He put the laptop aside and proceeded to kiss her from the tips of her fingers to the top of her shoulder and then back down to her fingers again. It was the most romantic, thrilling thing Alicia had ever seen or felt.

CHAPTER 15

ON SUNDAY MORNING, Alicia logged in to the Amigas Inc. e-mail account and was pleased to see that Julia Centavo had already gotten back to them. She read over the e-mail and called both Carmen and Jamie on her parents' conference line.

"So, what did she say?" Jamie asked.

"She loves all of it," Alicia explained, "and so does her client. But they have a few requests. Apparently, the girl's favorite flowers are yellow sunflowers. So they'd like the room to be full of sunflowers."

Carmen groaned. "But we hate sunflowers."

Jamie agreed. "Sunflowers are not chic."

Alicia hated this part of the job—when you conceived of the perfect, absolutely flawless *quince* and the client ruined it by having a request that was either cornball cheesy or aesthetically misguided.

"Look," Alicia said diplomatically, "I think

sunflowers are fine for farms and country inns, but not city homes or formal parties. It is my least favorite flower in the entire world. But this is not my *quince*, and the client is always right. So, sunflowers it is."

"Okay, so much for loving all of our ideas," Jamie grumbled. "Well, really Gaz's and our ideas. Why did we ever let him quit the Amigas?"

"Because, one, he hated being part of a group called Amigas Inc., and, two, his music career is on fire," Alicia explained. "Speaking of which, they actually love Gaz's music, so he'll be the house band. Which is amazing. Tremendous exposure for him."

"Great, terrific," Jamie muttered. "So, tell me more about the terrible choices they've made. That's more interesting."

Alicia scanned the e-mail. "They don't like the color scheme."

Now it was Carmen's turn to be bent out of shape. "You're kidding me, right? Black, white, and hot pink is so, well, hot. It's more than hot, it's so totally high class it's *haute*."

Alicia rolled over in bed and read the e-mail more closely. "I know it's *haute*. You know it's *haute*. But they would like red, white, and blue. For obvious reasons, I guess."

Carmen was still not convinced. "I get it, she's a DC It Girl, and more power to her. But red, white, and blue in Miami? In December? It's going to look like we got all her *quince* gear at some Fourth of July clearance sale."

Alicia laughed, "I know, Carmen. That's neither hot nor *haute*. But we'll make it work. We always do."

Jamie piped up and asked, "Is there any more of this mayhem and foolishness?"

Alicia read down the list. "No church ceremony, too polarizing for this multicultural crowd. No *damas* and *chambelanes*, too much like the British monarchy, and the client needs to represent more democratic ideals."

"Give me a break!" Jamie barked. "Why don't they just come out and admit that it's Carmela Ortega already?"

Alicia shrugged. "Who knows? She'll be bringing her own dress, so no crazy sewing for you, Carmen."

Carmen sniffed. "I kind of would love a crazy sewing job, especially if the dress might end up in the Smithsonian."

Alicia read further and told her friends, "This is odd, but she will be doing a father-daughter *vals*. But will not have time to work with a local choreographer. So she would like me to demonstrate the choreography with my own father, have someone videotape it, and e-mail it to her so she and her father can study it."

Jamie guffawed. "Wow. She's awfully bossy and specific for someone who won't reveal her identity. What's the song?"

Alicia read from the e-mail: "*Unfortunately, I cannot reveal the song that my client will dance to with her father as we would hate for the press to obtain this information. However, it will be a traditional* vals. *Speaking of which, we do hope that you will have every member of your team sign the enclosed confidentiality agreement and that you will return it to me at your earliest convenience.*"

Alicia sighed. "So that's it. The rest of this stuff is pretty standard, and she did go for the majority of our ideas. I should probably have a meeting with Carolina and Patricia to go over all of this."

Carmen jumped in. "You know what, Lici? Why don't you take the day off? You've put in so much time already. I can meet with Patricia and Carolina."

Alicia bit her lip remembering what her father always said about delegating. Come next fall, she wouldn't be there to supervise every step in the planning of the *quinces*. She had to start letting go. Entrances and exits, she reminded herself. Those were always the trickiest. Determined to turn over a new, more collaborative leaf, she agreed to let Carmen take the reins for a while.

Alicia knew that Sunday was Gaz's songwriting day. It was the only day of the week when he was neither in school nor at the Gap. He wouldn't answer the telephone while he was in the "lab," which was what he called the garage where he kept his instruments and recording equipment. But Alicia sent him a text: *c.g. loved your music. What can I say? the girl's got taste.*

Seconds later, he wrote back: *And I love you. What can I say? I've got taste.*

With an unusually free afternoon on her hands, Alicia showered and dressed and wandered into the kitchen at the very unseemly hour of eleven a.m.

"Good morning, *mija*," her mother said, kissing her on the forehead.

"You mean, good afternoon," her father joked.

Maribelle was at the stove making omelets.

Alicia gave her a hug. "I missed you yesterday," she said.

"Oh, yeah?" Maribelle sniffed. "That's why you made those disgusting waffles full of candy and sugar? People will think I taught you how to cook like that!"

Alicia winked at her mother and said, "Actually,

that's what I tell people. I also tell them that you're the one who taught me how to bake from box mixtures."

Maribelle looked scandalized. "Bake from a box? *¡Nunca en mi vida!*"

Alicia laughed. "Just kidding, just kidding."

Marisol Cruz spoke. "Hey, Alicia, you wouldn't have a couple of hours to lend your keen fashion eye, would you?"

Shopping? Alicia perked up. She loved to go shopping with her mother. Unfortunately, Marisol Cruz was usually so busy that her visits to the mall were few and far between.

"Actually, I'm free all day."

"Excellent," Marisol said. "Your father and I have a black-tie event next month, and I hate to sound like a cliché, but I have nothing I feel like wearing."

An hour later, Alicia and her mother were in side-by-side dressing rooms at their favorite South Beach boutique. Although Alicia had no need for a black-tie-event dress, her mother had encouraged her to pick out a stack of dresses to try on, so she could "keep her company."

In short order, Marisol Cruz fell hard for a black strapless sheath with an asymmetrical hemline that showed off her still gorgeous legs.

Alicia emerged from the dressing room in a silver-and-black-sequined minidress with bell sleeves.

"Look at you," her mother sighed. "You are a vision."

Alicia stared at herself in the mirror and wondered when exactly it was that she had grown up. She looked like the kind of girl whose pictures she still cut out of magazines and taped to the inside of her notebooks for inspiration. It was then that she realized that somewhere deep inside, she still saw herself as the fourteen-year-old kid with braces, practicing pop routines in front of her mirror, ready to storm the world and make everybody notice her. The girl she saw in the mirror, the girl in the sequined dress, didn't need to storm anything; the world—whatever part of it mattered—would come to *her*.

"You need to own that dress," her mother said. "It was made for you."

Alicia looked at the price tag and nearly choked. "Uh, no, this dress was made for someone like *you*, with a bunch of fancy degrees and a really good paycheck. But before I take it off, Mom," she asked, rummaging in her bag for her smart phone, "can you take a picture of me in it?"

Her mother whispered conspiratorially so that the saleswoman wouldn't hear them. "Are you thinking what I'm thinking? That Carmen could maybe do a copy of this dress?"

Alicia shook her head. "No, I don't need a copy of this dress. I don't even need this dress. I just want a picture of myself as a reminder of how grown-up I felt in this absolutely exquisite garment."

Her mother paused, and for a second, Alicia thought she was going to give her one of those "my little girl's all grown up" speeches. But Mrs. Cruz just took a deep breath, stepped back from her, and said, "Say, *'queso.'*" And Alicia did.

CHAPTER 16

A FEW WEEKS LATER, on a Saturday night, Alicia walked up to the door on Collins Avenue and looked dubiously at her friends. "I can't believe we're going bowling," she groaned, tugging at the shoulder of her very cute, very cropped, black leather jacket. "I haven't gone bowling since I was twelve."

"*And* Jamie said to dress cute," Carmen said. She was wearing one of her original designs: a studded black romper with sleek black tights. "Who dresses cute to go bowling?"

Jamie, who was decked out in a military green silk romper and hot pink pumps, put a hand up and said, "Stop the noise! This place is off the chain, you'll see. I just got a text from Dash. The guys are already inside."

The Amigas walked into Lucky Strike Lanes and Lounge and were surprised to see a room that looked more like a nightclub than any bowling alley they'd ever seen. Giant black-and-white prints hung against one wall, while cherrywood tables and sleek velvet wraparound couches practically screamed, *Sit. Hang. Relax.* Which is exactly what Gaz, Dash, and Maxo were doing.

Alicia walked over to Gaz and gave him a peck on the cheek. She wanted to give him a bigger kiss, but for some reason, she felt silly being overly affectionate in front of her friends. Maybe because she and Gaz had been the first in their group to get together, she had always felt the need to be low-key, so that the fact that they were a couple wouldn't affect her friendships with Carmen and Jamie.

Jamie, in contrast, felt no such compunctions. Partly because Dash was away at college and came home to visit only infrequently, and partly because the two of them were so newly and crazily in love, she walked right up to him, jumped on his lap, and proceeded to give him a kiss that was as sexy as something out of a music video.

"Hello! You're not alone in this lounge!" Alicia commented, looking up briefly from the e-mail message she was typing furiously into her iPad.

Jamie unfastened her lips from Dash's and sat back with a satisfied grin. "Look, *chica*, it's not every day that my guy comes home for Thanksgiving vacation."

"Well, the rest of us would be mighty thankful if you would save your making out for more private moments," Alicia said, her eyes now glued to her e-mail.

"Relax, Lici," Carmen said. "We don't mind if Dash and Jamie engage in PDA; it's cheaper than cable TV."

Carmen and Maxo held hands quietly. They were, as usual, sweetly in love but ultra laid-back about it.

"In fact, your boyfriend wouldn't mind some of that attention," Gaz hinted, tugging at Alicia's arm. "What are you doing?"

Alicia continued to look down at her iPad. "Sorry, I'm just totally and completely stressed about the mystery *quince*."

"Is there a problem with the planning?" Gaz asked.

Jamie jumped in. "No. Carolina and Patricia are doing an amazing job. It's just that our control-freak leader is having trouble letting go."

Carmen took the iPad from Alicia. "Since you're not going to be able to stop thinking about it, why don't we do a quick review of the checklist?"

The guys looked disappointed.

"I thought this was supposed to be a date," Dash protested, "not a meeting of Amigas Inc."

Jamie patted his shoulder reassuringly. "Look at

this place! It's incredible. Why don't you guys go and bowl one game and we'll join in on the next one? We just have to do a little *quince*-zilla intervention and then we'll be good to go."

Dash smiled and stood up. "That sounds like a plan. Though I have to warn you guys, I am a professional baller."

Gaz and Maxo exchanged amused glances. "And that means what, exactly?" Maxo asked.

"I'm a champion athlete," Dash boasted. "I tend to win at most recreational sports involving opaque objects of a circular nature."

Gaz guffawed. "You do know that bowling is done with a big black ball, not a tiny, preppy, country-club white ball, right?"

Dash nodded. "Of course."

"Okay, then," Gaz said. "Prepare to go down." Then he turned to kiss Alicia on the forehead. "See you in a few."

Now that the guys were gone and Jamie was back from the bar with a round of Scarlet Palmer mocktails, the girls got down to business.

Carmen had opened the Amigas Inc. checklist on her iPad.

"The site is sorted," she said.

Alicia piped up, "But maybe we should be thinking about someplace around here. I mean, how do you have a quintessential Miami *quince* and not have it in South Beach?"

Jamie rolled her eyes. "The *quince* is at Chez Gusteau. That's it. Done."

Carmen moved on and confirmed that the *amigas* had videotaped the choreography for the father-daughter *vals*, booked Gaz's band for the music, ordered the flowers as requested, and set a menu for the evening.

Alicia did not look convinced. "But what about the cake tasting?"

"We've already booked the Libalele Bakery to make Carmela's favorite red velvet cupcakes," Carmen replied.

Alicia shook her head. "We're going to need additional tables and chairs. Also, the chairs need to have white cotton slipcovers."

Carmen looked down at the list. "Carolina and Patricia have already done it."

Alicia jumped up. "It would be really nice if the slipcovers had a cluster of tiny stars embroidered on them."

Carmen tapped on the iPad and pulled up a picture of a chair covered in a white slipcover with a delicate star pattern embroidered on the fabric. "The Reinoso girls have already done it," she explained.

But Alicia, who was clearly working herself into a frenzy, only got more upset. "Wait a second. I didn't approve embroidered slipcovers. You know, just because her mother is a VIP and they are spending a packet on this *quince* does NOT mean that we can go over budget. I'm worried about Carolina and Patricia. They aren't responsible enough to lead Amigas Inc. I'm going to have to go to a state school and make sure they don't run the business into the ground."

Jamie turned off the iPad and said, "Enough already. You are flipping out. Carolina and Patricia are doing a great job. You not only approved the budget for the embroidered slipcovers, it was your idea—as demonstrated by the fact that you just had the same idea five minutes ago. We've planned two dozen *quinces* over the last two years, and while we've had our share of *dama* drama, mama drama, and makes-me-wanna-holla drama, we haven't had one unhappy customer on the actual big day. It all works out. We do good work. And I'm pretty sure that Carmela's *quince* will be no exception."

Carmen took her friend's hand and gave it a squeeze. "Jamie's right, Alicia. It's all going to work out. Everything is set. The only thing that you should be worrying about is the little details that would make this *quince* extra special. You're the *best* at those ideas. So, if anything occurs to you, anything at all, e-mail Carolina and Patricia, and CC me and Jamie. We will make sure that it happens."

The girls finished their drinks and stood up. Jamie said, "Let's bowl, *chicas.*"

Alicia looked down at her high-heeled black leather booties. "I can't believe that I wore these shoes to go bowling in."

"You didn't," Jamie said, leading the way down the neon-lit hall. "You wore those shoes to look cute in the lounge. For the actual bowling, you have to wear bowling shoes."

They stood at the counter in front of a wall of cubbies filled with bowling shoes. Carmen studied the design of the shoe appreciatively. "These are actually more like cute oxfords than the clown shoes I remember from when we were kids," she observed. "I totally approve."

Each girl asked an employee for her size and changed shoes. Then they went to find the boys.

In lane number five, Dash was throwing his bowling ball in a unique—and off-balance—way while the other guys watched.

"Who's winning?" Alicia asked, giving Gaz a big hug.

"I am," he said, proudly.

Dash scowled playfully. "Those balls are heavier than they look."

Maxo winked at Gaz. "And for some reason, Dash's ball has a pesky habit of falling into the gutter."

Jamie reset the game. "Okay, ixnay on that game. New game. Amigas Inc. versus Los Hombres. And I'm up first."

After she got home that night, Alicia changed into her favorite pajamas and brushed out her hair. She was surprised that she'd spent her Saturday night bowling and also that the place had been so cool. She took out her iPad and began to e-mail her friends:

To: Carmen, Jamie
From: Alicia
Subject: Future *Quinces*

Hey, *chicas*, Feeling much calmer. Thanks for talking me off the ledge. The Lucky Strike Lanes and Lounge was as fab as promised. We should do a *quince* there someday.

She checked the Amigas Inc. in-box, responded to messages, and started to think about what would make Carmela Ortega's *quince* extra special.

To: Carolina, Patricia
Cc: Carmen, Jamie
From: Alicia
Subject: Mass book

Although Carmela Ortega is not having a church
ceremony, it might be nice to do a little booklet of
inspiring words and prayers as a keepsake for her
and her guests.

Eager to take her mind off the *quince* planning,
Alicia picked up a copy of *Teen Vogue* and flipped to an
article about yearbook photos. Immediately, her mind
went into high gear.

To: Carolina, Patricia
Cc: Carmen, Jamie
From: Alicia
Subject: *Quince* portrait

I cannot believe that we forgot to schedule a
photographer and a location for Carmela's *quince*
portrait. We need to talk wardrobe, hair and
makeup, and photographer. Let's get on this first
thing in the morning, people!

Alicia turned off the iPad and turned out the lights. But five minutes later, she sat up with a jolt and, once again, reached for the iPad.

To: Carolina, Patricia
Cc: Carmen, Jamie
From: Alicia
Subject: Animal wrangler

We've never done a live dove release. But this is an element that is very popular at weddings. We should look into it, as doves symbolize peace, and Carmela's mother has been so involved in peacemaking efforts abroad.

P.S. Am I the only one who is thinking out of the box about this *quince*?

Alicia was just about to go to sleep, or try to, when she saw that she had four new messages.

The e-mail from Carolina read: *On it, boss.*

Patricia had written: *I think the doves might be a bit much. Let's discuss.*

Carmen's message said: *Try to relax, Lici.*

And Jamie, as ever, had gotten straight to the point: *GO TO BED, LOCA!*

Alicia took a deep breath and wrote a reply.

To: Carolina, Patricia
Cc: Carmen, Jamie
From: Alicia
Subject: Just one more thing

I agree that doves might be a little much. And I
am going to bed very soon. I just had one more
thought. What about butterflies? What if the entire
dining room was filled with butterflies? Wouldn't
that be beautiful?

Content that she'd done all that she could about
the planning, Alicia hit SEND and turned out the lights
once more.

Five minutes later, her cell phone rang. It was Jamie.
It was one o'clock in the morning.

"Hey Jamie, are you all right?" Alicia asked, truly
concerned.

"I am fine," said her friend, on the other end of the
line. "But you won't be if you keep e-mailing us your
late-night musings. Go to bed, Alicia. Or we'll vote you
off the island."

CHAPTER 17

THE MORNING OF December 15, Alicia awoke extra early. She always got up without an alarm on *quince* day. Whether it was nerves or just the early-bird planner in her, she could never sleep late on the day of a *quince*. Today was a big day. She was finally going to meet her most illustrious client yet, Carmela Ortega, as well as her mother, Yesenia, and the family's personal secretary, Julia Centavo.

The day before, the partners of Amigas Inc. and their successors, Carolina and Patricia, had done a walk-through at the restaurant. Alicia had cringed when she saw the red, white, and blue plates and tablecloths that the Ortegas had chosen and the big, rustic vases full of sunflowers that filled the restaurant's pantry area. But she reminded herself that their job as *quince* planners was to make each girl's dream come true, not dictate what those dreams should be.

Not that there was any possibility of bossing the Ortegas around. In addition to being very specific about their wishes, they were also still keeping many aspects of the *quince* a secret. Alicia and her team had not even gotten a glimpse of the guest list. Once the invitations were printed, they were mailed to a PO box in Fairfax, Virginia, where Julia Centavo saw to it that they were addressed by hand (by an expensive calligrapher) and mailed out in the most confidential manner possible.

For nearly a month, Alicia and her father had been rehearsing a father-daughter *vals* while her mother filmed them so that the *amigas* could show their ideas to the client. Alicia tried to keep the choreography simple, but the client kept requesting more and more changes in the dance routine. More than once, Alicia had had to fight the temptation to stick her tongue out at the camera. As it was, she was a little afraid that the camera might have captured an involuntary roll of her eyes. But really, she didn't mind. Her father was a good dancer. And they had fun improvising insane, never-to-be-seen-by-the-public father-daughter dances like one they called the Drunken Monkey.

For security reasons, the Amigas Inc. team was not allowed to arrive at the event until half an hour before the guests were due. In the world of party-planners, this was absolutely unheard-of. While Alicia sincerely hoped that everything would go off without a hitch, she half expected to get a panicky call on her cell phone from Julia Centavo, begging her to come over to the restaurant and deal with some last-minute catastrophe.

Carolina and Patricia had assembled Welcome to Miami gift baskets complete with art deco beach towels, palm-tree-shaped cookies, and little boxes of coconut water. But since Ms. Centavo wouldn't reveal—again for security purposes—the name of the hotel where out-of-town guests were staying, the Reinoso girls had been directed to deliver those baskets at noon to the restaurant, where a member of the security detail would inspect them and make sure they got to the hotel. Alicia had always loved preparing the welcome baskets, and while she knew it was a good task to delegate, she missed being a part of organizing those last-minute finishing touches that truly made an event special.

The client had taken Amigas Inc.'s suggestion for a local hairstylist and makeup artist. Sonja Sinski, Alicia's favorite hairstylist, was being picked up at three o'clock and taken to the guest of honor's hotel suite. Julia Centavo had also hired Myra Abney, Alicia's favorite makeup artist, who had a knack for making you look as though you were wearing no makeup at all.

Alicia had been especially pleased that the Ortegas had taken her hair and makeup suggestions. Nothing made a *quince* feel worse than being tended to for hours, then looking up and realizing that her hair and makeup were so overdone she felt more like the Bride of Frankenstein than like a beautiful birthday girl.

Since Carmen did not have to make any outfits for Carmela's event, she had taken the lead on all the food and beverages. She planned to head straight to the restaurant to make sure that everything was as ordered and that the desserts, especially the mini pineapple-upside-down cakes, would come off without a hitch.

Jamie was busy working on backdrops and sets. Alicia was excited to see the portraits of all the guests posed in front of stylishly designed murals featuring planes, yachts, and cars.

And Gaz, while nervous, was excited to be performing for what was certain to be an illustrious crowd.

Alicia knew she wouldn't see him until half an hour before the event. She went over her checklist twice. Then, having sincerely intended to delegate, she sent out reminder texts, letting everybody know what he or she was supposed to be managing and that they should all call her if they needed any help at all.

Carolina wrote back: *We're good, boss.*

Patricia texted: *You are going to be so proud of us, you may take the rest of the year off.*

Alicia laughed and thought, *Yeah, right.*

Carmen texted: *Relax, Lici. You do know the meaning of that word, right?*

Gaz wrote simply: *I'll be singing to you tonight.*

He always said that. "No matter how many people are in the room," he would tell her when she went to see him perform, "remember, I'm only singing to you."

In response to Alicia's message asking whether all was well with the sets, Jamie texted a picture of a beautiful mural depicting a yacht and asked: *Hey, bossy, does this float your boat?*

Alicia laughed and wrote back: *Yes, gorgeous. Good job.*

Alicia had been e-mailing Julia Centavo every hour on the hour to make sure that everything was going okay, and every response came back the same: *Yes, it's all great. Looking forward to meeting you.* Alicia couldn't believe it. For the first time in forever, she was not crazed on *quince* day. In fact, the process was actually running itself.

Determined to use her free time wisely, Alicia pulled out a sheet of paper and began to write her college essay. There were more false starts than she would have liked, but by late afternoon, she thought she had managed to capture exactly what she wanted to say to the college admissions committee at Harvard and all the other schools where she was applying.

The Day I Would Live Over
By Alicia Cruz

In January 1959, my mother's parents fled Cuba and moved to Miami. In February 1959, my father's parents made the same journey. A few years later, living in a poverty their parents could never have imagined, each family welcomed a child. My mother was born an American, a poor American, but an American all the same. My father was also born an American and a proud one. He always says that his citizenship was the only trust fund he ever needed.

Growing up in Miami, I have been surrounded by the swirl of Spanish and English and the vast realm of language that lives in between. I go to school with kids of every different color, on a campus that actually has an ocean view. I am an inveterate city girl who has a country girl's appreciation of nature due to the palm trees and beaches that are part of my natural habitat.

Although my two best girlfriends are Latina, I never thought too deeply about my heritage. It was a fact, a part of me, the same way that I know without thinking about it that I have dark hair and brown eyes. And while I love Latin music and Latin food, I have to admit that I often thought of Latin culture as something yellow and crumbling, like the trunk full of <u>Life</u> magazines my abuelo keeps in the basement.

In Latin culture, girls celebrate the quinceañera, or Sweet Fifteen, instead of the American Sweet Sixteen. This is a tradition that goes back hundreds of years to a time when Latin countries were synonymous with great civilizations and great discoveries—not with poverty and ecotourism and the drug trade. A quince wears a crown because it is a tradition that links her to the highest royal courts, but I didn't know all of that when I was fourteen, about to turn fifteen. I thought having a quince was about expensive parties and <u>Gone with the Wind</u>-style dresses, and I thought it wasn't for me. So when my parents offered me a choice, I chose to go to Spain with my dear friend Carmen. And, while exploring the streets of Barcelona is a marvelous way to turn fifteen, it is not a quince.

Then, two years ago, I met a girl who was new to Miami and—long story—I helped her plan her quince. That quince led to another and another, and before we knew it, my friends and I had a bona fide business. And what I have learned over the last two years is that my culture is a living, breathing thing. It is not an old magazine in my grandfather's basement, nor is it a lost jewel, flung into the ocean in the stretches of sea between where my grandparents were born and where my parents and I were raised. To be a Latina is an exciting, modern thing, and, while I understand that now, regret is useless. If I had one day to live over, I would go back to my fifteenth birthday and I would throw a party for my family and friends—not to get presents, not to parade around in a dress, but to say, this is who I am, this is where I came from, and this is where I hope to go.

Alicia's cell phone began ringing; she couldn't believe it: it was five thirty! She was going to be late for Carmela Ortega's *quinceañera*! All because she had gotten caught up in writing her college essay. She picked up the phone; it was Carmen.

"The car service has been parked outside of your house for an hour, Lici," Carmen said. "Didn't you hear the doorbell?" Alicia had been so busy writing (and blasting Shakira songs for inspiration) that she had not.

"What am I going to do?" Alicia could feel the tears coming as she confided to Carmen, "I'm not even dressed!"

Carmen sounded impatient. "Get dressed. Pronto. Gosh, Alicia, this is so not like you. What were you doing?"

"Working on my college essay," Alicia replied. "I think it's really good."

Carmen seemed to soften at the mention of the essay. She knew how important it was to Alicia.

"Well," Carmen said, "bring a copy of the essay. We can read it when everyone's having their sit-down." As a rule, Carmen, Jamie, and Alicia always waited until the guests were seated for the sit-down portion of their meal, then took their plates to some quiet corner and had a few minutes of food and recap before they were on and in full hostess mode again.

• • •

When the car service arrived at the restaurant, Alicia got out and stood for a few moments watching a plane take off into the sky. As many times as she herself had flown, as many times as she'd been to the airport to pick up and drop off family, friends, *quinces*, and guests, it always seemed to her a sort of miracle that a big hunk of metal could so elegantly take to the sky.

Carmen stood at the back door of the restaurant and called to her: "Hey, daydreamer, get to work!"

Alicia rushed inside. She was wearing a favorite work outfit: a navy blue smocked dress with a simple pleated skirt. She, Carmen, and Jamie always dressed down when they worked a party. You never ever wanted to steal a *quince*'s thunder.

Carmen led Alicia by the hand to the lounge downstairs. "There's someone I want you to meet," she said as they descended the staircase.

"Is it Carmela Ortega?" Alicia asked excitedly.

She saw a familiar figure emerge from behind a pillar. It was her mother, and she was holding *that* dress. "Pleased to meet you," said Marisol Cruz, extending her hand as if they were strangers. "I'm Julia Centavo."

At first, Alicia thought her mother was playing a joke. Was this just her clever way of treating her to a ridiculously gorgeous, absolutely expensive dress?

Then Jamie appeared and handed Alicia an envelope. She said, "I thought you might like to see the real invitation."

Alicia opened the envelope to see a white card with black and hot pink type. It read:

YOU ONLY *QUINCE* TWICE.
PLEASE JOIN US TO CELEBRATE THE BIRTHDAY
OF MIAMI'S *QUINCE* QUEEN:
ALICIA CRUZ

As Alicia held the invitation, her hands began to shake. How could it be? It was all so marvelous and unexpected and unreal. Once she started crying, she truly couldn't stop. Carmen and Jamie led her to a back room, where Sonja and Myra waited to do her hair and makeup.

"Stop the tears, diva!" Sonja called out in a sunny tone. "This is all about love. Relax and let it in."

Alicia listened to the words, repeated them in her head, and felt herself get calmer with every repetition: *This is all about love. Relax. Let it in. This is all about love. Relax. Let it in.*

Her mother helped her change into the dress, and

from the moment the material brushed her skin, she felt a little more grown-up, a little more able to deal with the fact that she'd been had, hoodwinked, bamboozled—in the best possible way, of course. But bamboozled all the same.

"But how . . . ?" she asked her mother and friends as she sat in the high chair and Sonja began to blow out her hair.

"You never had a *quince*," Carmen explained.

"And you, of all people, certainly deserve one," Jamie added. "Carmen and I were sitting and counting and we realized that Amigas Inc. had planned twenty-four *quinces* over the last two years. So we thought maybe we could make your party number twenty-five. We called your parents and they came up with the whole cloak-and-dagger routine."

"Well, we know how much you love James Bond movies," Alicia's mother explained.

Her father had joined the group, and the smile on his face was a mile wide. "I can't believe you never got it. 'Julia Centavo' is almost a literal translation of 'Jane Moneypenny,' the secretary to M, Bond's boss, the head of the British Secret Service! And you're a girl who got a nearly perfect score on her SATs," he teased.

Alicia was still feeling surprised. "So, who's on the

guest list?" she asked as Myra expertly applied the most natural-looking makeup.

"Well, it wouldn't be a surprise if we told you, would it?" her mother asked, squeezing her hand. "Are you ready to meet your public?"

Alicia nodded, and then, hand in hand with her mother as if she were a little girl, Alicia went back upstairs to the restaurant.

The first people she saw were Carolina and Patricia Reinoso, who were dressed alike in simple black shifts. "Hey, you never dress alike!" Alicia noted.

Carolina smiled, "We learned from the master. It's in the *quince* planning playbook. Never steal a *quince*'s thunder."

The room was packed, and the red, white, and blue tablecloths and the big jugs of sunflowers that had filled the room before were nowhere to be found. Each table was covered with a white tablecloth and a square black vase filled with hot pink roses and lilies.

Mr. Stevens was holding court at one table with all of Alicia's new friends from her Surfing the New Economy course. Alicia spotted her friends from Austin, Valeria and her parents. Carmen's family were at one table. Jamie's, including her extended family from New York, occupied another. Gaz's mother was sitting at a table with Alicia's *Abuelo* and *Abuela* Cruz and Mrs. Cruz's parents, Nana and Papi Velasquez.

Alicia was walking around half in a daze, hugging and greeting people, when her mother said, "Lici, your court is waiting for you."

Mrs. Cruz led her to the courtyard, where a small formal court awaited her. The *damas* were Carmen, Jamie, Sarita—the very first girl whose *quince* Alicia had planned—and Binky Mortimer. They were all dressed in beautiful hot pink dresses. Carmen said, "And you said there was no sewing for this *quince*! A fat lot you knew!"

The *chambelanes* were in black tie, led by her ever dapper, unbelievably handsome boyfriend, Gaz. She kissed him quickly and shyly.

"You knew?" she whispered.

He laughed, "Oh, Alicia, *everyone* knew but you."

The other *chambelanes* were Dash, Maxo, and Alicia's brother, Alex.

She gave her brother a huge hug. "Wait a second; you came all the way from Montreal for this?" she asked.

"Of course," her brother replied. "Well, it's not every day that your sister has a *quinceañera*, especially one that's years behind schedule."

Flustered, Alicia looked over to Carmen and Jamie. "What do I do? We never rehearsed anything!" She had supervised the entrance of many courts. Now it was her turn, and she could barely put one foot in front of another.

The *damas* and *chambelanes* lined up single file, with Alicia in the very back. Then, as Gaz began to sing a sweet a cappella version of "Do You Know Where You're Going To?" they walked slowly into the restaurant.

When they were all inside, Jamie addressed the crowd: "Ladies and gentlemen, I present to you Alicia Cruz."

Alicia stepped forward. "I don't have any prepared remarks," she said. "As you all know, this whole thing is a bit of a surprise. But because I believe in fate, I wanted to read you my college application essay, which I wrote today, when I thought that tonight we would be cele-brating someone else entirely. I just need to run and get my bag in the kitchen. I'll be right back."

As quickly as she could in three-inch heels, she sprinted into the kitchen, soon returning with the print-out. She felt nerves churning her stomach as she began reading, but after the first few sentences, she was able to calm down and focus on the words. As she spoke, she looked around the room at all of the people who had done so much to plan this night: her parents, Gaz, the *amigas*. She felt like the luckiest *chica* in the world.

By the time she was finished reading, Carmen and Jamie were sniffling, and Alicia's parents and grandparents were all weeping.

"Hey, everybody, can I have your attention?" Jamie called out. "In lieu of the traditional father-daughter *vals*, I want to show you a short film I've been working on. Please join me in the garden, and bring your tissues, because I can almost guarantee there will be more crying."

Projected on a large screen, where "Julia Centavo" had requested that they show *Breakfast at Tiffany's* after dinner, there was a photo that Alicia remembered from preschool days. It showed her, dressed in an orange T-shirt and pink tutu, teaching her father how to dance ballet as he, dressed in a suit and tie, gamely tried to do a plié. This was followed by a series of cherished home videos and pictures that the Cruz family had accumulated over the years. All of a sudden, Alicia realized why her mother had taken all those videos of her and her father rehearsing the father-daughter *vals*. She had captured every laugh, every side glance, every silly moment, as well as their rendition of the Drunken Monkey. Jamie had edited the film together beautifully and set it to Stevie Wonder's "Isn't She Lovely?" This was the song her father had been singing to her ever since she was a baby, just home from the hospital.

As the movie was playing, Alicia happened to catch a glimpse of Mr. Stevens. He extended his arms, as if he were riding a big wave. She mimicked his gesture. He liked to say that in surfing, as in business, and as in life, it didn't matter how many times you fell—it mattered only how often you were willing to stand up. She looked around the restaurant garden, at the room filled with people whom she loved and who loved her in return. She did not know what exactly was ahead. It was almost certain that she would experience her share of wipeouts, as all the best surfers did. But it didn't matter, because tonight, she was most definitely standing up.

EPILOGUE

FIVE MONTHS LATER, the *amigas* met up at the Lucky Strike Lanes and Lounge once again. Alicia, Jamie, and Carmen sat on one side of a leather banquette, Patricia and Carolina on the other. Gaz and Dash were battling furiously in the lanes as Maxo looked on from the sidelines, amused.

Gaz, handsome in a white linen shirt and khakis, lifted his bowling ball in an elaborate, show-offy pose, then proceeded to bowl his fifth strike in a row. "See, Dash," he crowed, "*¡Así, se hace!*"

Dash pretended to look crestfallen. "I just don't get it. How can I tear it up on the golf course and fail so miserably at a nonsport like bowling?"

But Gaz was far from through with him. "That's your problem, hombre. Your elitism is hanging you up. You gotta humble yourself for the game, 'cause this 'nonsport' is kicking your booty!"

Maxo nodded in agreement. "I think my man here has a point."

In the lounge area behind the lanes, the *chicas* weren't paying attention to the boys or their rivalry. A waitress delivered plates of nachos and smoothies to the candlelit table, and the girls dived in.

"I can't believe it's already May," Alicia exclaimed, incredulous that their senior year was almost over. She was rocking a very cute pale pink T-shirt dress that looked kind of fabulous with her funky tan bowling shoes.

"Totally. I mean, it seems like just yesterday that we had you entirely believing that we were planning a *quinceañera* for the ambassador to Mexico's daughter," Jamie teased. She was wearing a crisp white shirt, one of Dash's ties, and a fitted navy blazer and navy shorts.

Carmen gave her best friend a hug. "Little did you know that we had a much more important, much more fabulous client—namely, you!"

Alicia sat up straight. "And I love you all for lying to me, deceiving me, and giving me the most memorable *quince* ever. Speaking of which, as of September, Carolina and Patricia will officially take over as codirectors of Amigas Inc. And in honor of their—*ahem*—ascension, we have a little present."

Alicia reached into her bag and pulled out two custom-made tiaras. The words *Amigas Inc.* were written in silver script atop a feathery pink base. She handed a crown to each of the Reinoso girls.

"Love it!" Carolina cried, immediately putting on her crown.

True to her edgier style, Patricia first mussed up her hair, then put her crown on, so that it tilted to one side like a fedora. "I think that I might dye the feathers black," she mused, "so it's much more downtown. Then I think I will wear it everywhere. *Gracias, chicas.*"

"So, how many *quinces* have we lined up for the summer?" Jamie asked Alicia.

Alicia threw her hands up in the air. "I swear, being so good at our jobs is a blessing and a curse."

"Meaning . . . ?" Jamie pressed.

"Meaning that we've got six *quinces* on the books between now and August fifth, when we've got to leave for freshman orientation," Alicia explained.

"I'm kind of bummed about being a freshman all over again," Jamie complained. "Once we got through the madness of SATs, college applications, and planning Lici's *quince*, being a senior kind of rocked."

Dash, Gaz, and Maxo joined the group, and Dash said, "Being a freshman is not so bad. Especially since you'll be at Stanford in sunny California with your boyfriend, who'll be a sophomore transfer student."

Alicia and Carmen were still in shock that their Jamie—South Bronx Jamie, boogie-down Jamie, graffiti-art-and-Jackson-Pollock-loving Jamie—was dating a champion golf player and was planning on majoring in East Asian studies and attending Stanford. But if there was one thing that planning twenty-five *quinceañeras* had taught the partners of Amigas Inc., it was this: it really was a girl's prerogative to change her mind.

Carmen, in contrast, was the definition of tried-and-true. Since she'd first seen an episode of *Project Runway* in junior high, she'd wanted to go to New York to study fashion design. And now, here she was, on her way to Parsons School of Design, and none of the others in the original Amigas Inc.—Alicia, Jamie, or Gaz—nor either of the new *amigas*—Patricia or Carolina—had any doubt that they would someday be able to walk into a store and buy the latest Carmen Ramirez-Ruben design.

Alicia was headed for Harvard, ready to follow in her parents' footsteps academically, but also ready to blaze her own trail as an entrepreneur. She'd had coffee several times with Serena Shih, the Harvard rep who'd initially gotten her interested in the joint BA/MBA program, and she was excited at the thought of spending her freshman year developing what she thought might be her first big project: an Amigas Inc. *quince* planning kit that could be sold nationwide.

Gaz sat next to her, whispering flirtatious things in her ear. She vacillated between wanting him to continue and fearing that she was blushing so hard everyone could tell what he was saying to her. Gaz had received and accepted a full scholarship to MIT, just a T train ride away from Alicia's campus at Harvard.

Alicia could hardly believe how many adventures she and her friends had experienced since they'd first decided to do a good deed and help a new girl in town plan her *quince*. It seemed fitting that they were all meeting up at a place called Lucky Strike, because it had indeed been lucky that they had all met, that they had become friends, that they had started a business together that had just kept growing. None of the original Amigas Inc. members were fifteen-year-olds anymore, but a *quinceañera* was about so much more than the number of candles on the cake. A *quince* was about becoming a woman. And in that definition of the term, Jamie, Alicia, and Carmen were all still very much in the midst of the party. And as Alicia looked at her friends, she could only hope that the growing up, and all the fun that went with it, would go on and on.

A Chat With
Jennifer Lopez

When I first came up with the idea for the Amigas series, I thought about the many Latina women who, like Alicia, Jamie, and Carmen, had started out as entrepreneurial teenagers. Who, through hard work, imagination, and dedication, were able to take their passions and talents and become role models and successful adults. For me, Jennifer Lopez is such a woman. She has incredible drive and an amazing work ethic, qualities she shares with the girls in Amigas. They, too, needed an equal amount of determination to turn their quince-party-planning business into a huge success.

So, to get a better sense of this connection, I sat down with Jennifer, and we talked about quinces and what it was like for her as a Latina girl growing up in New York City. Here are some more of her answers. . . .

—J. Startz

1. When you were a senior in high school, did you have a clear sense of what you wanted to pursue as a career in the future?

I didn't know exactly what I was going to pursue, but I did know that I loved to dance and to perform in front of an audience, as I had already done a couple of musical plays at the Kips Bay Boys & Girls Club and at my high school in the Bronx.

2. What extracurricular activity did you participate in that helped you zero in on what interested you the most?

I took up dancing and starred in a couple of plays in high school and at the Kips Bay Boys & Girls Club, a local community organization for kids that had a performing arts program in New York.

3. What would you say to teenagers who develop a passion for a particular career interest at an early age? Through your own personal experience, what advice would you offer them as to how to nourish and excel in their passion?

My advice would be to study hard and try to become the best at what you want to do.